Georgie Rivers
and the Cursed Caves

ROBERT EVANS

Copyright © 2018 Robert Evans

All characters in this publication are fictitious and any resemblance to real persons, living or dead, is purely coincidental.

All rights reserved.

Cover design by Robert Evans
Stock images licensed from istockphoto.com

For updates find @GeorgieRiversUK on Twitter
ISBN: 9781720294238

This book was written for my children L, N and R.
Without their inspiration & encouragement, Georgie Rivers wouldn't exist.

CONTENTS

	About the Author	i
1	Fresh Start	1
2	Family Secret	Pg 17
3	Northgate	Pg 32
4	Trouble on Two Sticks	Pg 46
5	Discoveries in the Dark	Pg 59
6	The Dragon's Eye	Pg 74
7	Taking a Risk	Pg 87
8	In Pursuit of Danger	Pg 106
9	Breaking and Entering	Pg 122
10	An Empty House	Pg 137
11	The Climb	Pg 154
12	Opening the Door	Pg 165
13	The Cursed Caves	Pg 175
14	New Beginnings	Pg 191

ABOUT THE AUTHOR

ROBERT EVANS has worked in the Post-production industry for many years, working on both television and feature films in the role of a Finishing Editor. His debut novel 'Georgie Rivers and the Cursed Caves' was inspired by his children and their love of a good story. He lives in South Wales with his family.

CHAPTER ONE
FRESH START

Waves crashed against rocky cliffs, as the wind howled hard and fast driving the rain. It was night-time, and the coastline was volatile and unrelenting. Two figures were barely visible from the brow of the cliff above, where a Land Rover Defender was parked with the driver sat inside. Chained together by rope for safety and clutching onto their flashlights with one hand and whatever surface they could with the other, the two men fought to see in front of them. They slowly but valiantly clawed their way toward a large hole in the side of the cliff face. A tall powerfully built man at the front stopped and turned his flashlight to the floor, he flashed it off and on four times. Seeing this, the body behind came to a swift halt. The second figure was slim and nimble and easily half the weight of the leader. He quickly turned around and got jolted back and forth as the huge man in front ripped open his backpack to retrieve what looked like sticks of dynamite from inside. With a red flash of smoke, flares were struck and thrown into the entrance of a cave. As the flares danced over the stone ground, they illuminated an ancient lobby of stalactites hanging from a huge cavernous ceiling.

The two men walked in further and removed their hoods and goggles and took in with awe the spectacle of what they were seeing. They dropped their bags and loosened the rope binding them. Dominik Carver reached into his jacket pocket and pulled out an old folded piece of parchment, he unraveled it while eagerly looking around the cave. Dutch, the larger of the two men continued to throw flares around the cave, lighting it up like it was almost daylight. He then started to build a fire in the corner, shielded from the wind. Dominik pointed his torch at the old paper and began to look at the markings and symbols drawn in faded black ink. Over the noise of the waves and wind outside, he shouted instructions to Dutch, his thick French accent filled the cave.

'Look around and see if you can see this symbol anywhere!'

Dominik held up the parchment and shone his flashlight at the paper, the symbol was that of a cross with a decorative circular pattern surrounding it. Dutch nodded and ignited his torch as they both silently got to work, checking every inch of the cave as quickly and thoroughly as they could.

Sat in the Land Rover safe from the extremities, awaited a woman in her late thirties. She rubbed at the condensation building up on the windscreen of the car, but it was no help, the rain outside was far too heavy for her to see anything. She took a pen out of the glove box and proceeded to attempt the half completed cross word on the back of the newspaper that she found on the back seat. It was two days out of date and the headlines read 'The Berlin Wall Crumbles'. She found the crossword child's play and completed it with the last clue being the word 'adventure', she smiled and filled in the eight boxes with the word escapade. It had been close to four hours since she sent her men to investigate the hole they saw in the cliff face earlier that day, from the safety of the boat they hired to trail the coast line. She glanced at her watch, an old diamond encrusted Omega handed down from her aunt, who had raised her in East Berlin. She was separated from her parents when Germany got divided into the east and west by the western allies and Russia. She thought of her every time she looked at it and how now, after so many years, her Aunt's promises could finally and hopefully come true. It was 3am, she took one last look outside before starting to consider firing up the engine and heading back into town. Thinking her men must have failed in the weather, she threw down the newspaper and reached for the keys. Suddenly the door of the Land Rover teared open and the newspaper got sucked outside into the heavy rain. Dutch threw an injured Dominik Carver into the car, clutching at his ankle and soaked from head to toe. He looked Madeline Wolf in the eye while clenching his teeth in pain and simply said 'Madame, we have found the caves'.

The dust on the windowsill was slowly getting soaked by drops of condensation running down the inside of the window. Georgie Rivers watched the water run down the pane of single glazed glass, occasionally striking through them with her finger to stop them reaching the windowsill below. Today was a difficult day, it was her last day at 33 Prestbury Hill and she was going to miss it dearly. Downstairs she could hear her father discussing their immediate plans to Mr and Mrs Weaver from number twelve across the road. They were an elderly couple and kind neighbours who had been hugely supportive for Georgie over the last two years, when her dad couldn't be. She didn't have any grandparents of her own and the Weavers made her feel safe and at home around them. Mrs Weaver would help Georgie with her homework and regularly encouraged her to help with baking cakes for her dad. Georgie would pretend to dislike baking profusely but secretly enjoyed it nearly as much as Mrs Weaver, who drank in the joy of having a child around the house, especially a girl.

Mr Weaver to Georgie was far more interesting than homework and cake baking. He would be happy to share an exciting story of when he was seventeen years old and serving in World War 2, working the supply train with mules and horses covering the African deserts and the jungles of Burma. Nearing seventy years old, but incredibly well for his age. Mr Weaver never failed to keep Georgie enthralled in an exciting tale of the time he saved one of his mules from being shot directly in the head by using a nearby frying pan as a shield. Or when he rode his favourite horse directly toward a German SS soldier, leaping over his head to avoid getting shot. She always wondered if Mr Weaver was completely honest with her about his stories. But she didn't care. He took her to a more exciting place, far away from the war she was fighting at home.

Georgie knew it was time to say goodbye to her old bedroom, she was going to miss the slanted ceiling where you could still see the marks of her glow in the dark stars and planets that were once tacked securely to the artex with blu tack. The removal men had packed everything early that morning while she sat on a stool eating her breakfast trying to stay out of the way. The carpet was exposed now and she ran her foot along the deep grooves of where her furniture used to stand. She then swept her hand along the cool papered walls that were once littered with posters of Nik Kershaw, a-ha and Duran Duran. Which she only put up to try to feel more 'normal' for her friend's sake more than hers. She walked out onto the landing and glanced at the three doors in front of her. Old mahogany doors with decades of layers of paint covering them, with chips on the sides revealing the various colours of the past owners' decorative tastes. She took one last big breath, closed her eyes, then opened them taking in each door as she turned her head. The spare room, bathroom and her parent's bedroom. Standing on the landing she could still hear the beep of the syringe driver that helped keep her mother comfortable for the last few weeks of her life. Continually feeding medication into her system, the alarm would ring when it needed attention. Her dad being a doctor had its benefits, allowing her mother to be at home rather than in the hospital. At the top of the stairs Georgie could hear the conversation clearly in the hallway below.

'Here's our new address and here's our new phone number, it's all set up'

'OK love, how's she doing?'

'Better than me, I can't thank you both enough for your help. She's going to miss you so much, I just hope I'm doing the right thing.'

Georgie's dad Thomas had been the town's youngest and most promising GP. He'd managed to keep himself and the house together as best he could, considering the circumstances. After nursing her mother for over a year and working part time, he needed to stop and rest and had suggested to Georgie that they move back to his hometown. He knew he was asking a lot of her after the torment they had been through, but she knew a fresh start was what they both needed, and her dad still had close friends there. Georgie on the other hand had discovered exactly who her friends were after her mum's illness and was more than happy to abandon them in favour of someone new. Being a twelve year old girl was never the easiest, especially if you were more interested in exploring, rock climbing, BMX riding and metal detecting rather than just listening to new romantics and talking about makeup.

Thomas turned his head around to see Georgie walking down the stairs, he smiled and held out his arm to comfort her to his side. She looked down at the Warwick

Victorian tiles under her feet, already missing them and wondered what the new house would be like. Mrs Weaver grabbed Georgie and gave her a tight hug.

'Come here you, whenever you want to chat we're just a phone call away, you know we don't go far. Especially with Captain Slow here.'

Mr Weaver pointed to his chest with his mouth open, pretending to be in shock. Georgie laughed into Mrs Weaver's shoulder, squeezed her back trying desperately not to make the single tear running down her cheek turn into more. Mrs Weaver struggled to hold back her tears also as she stepped back for Georgie's dad to close and lock the door for the last time. It was late autumn, yet the sun was warm on Georgie's face as she walked toward their car, the crisp brown leaves of the surrounding oak trees crunched under her trainers. She glanced back at the house one last time and said goodbye. Memories of her mother flooded her thoughts making her feel heavy in her chest and she ached to have her back. Waiting by the driver's side of the car her dad was struggling too. He smiled at Georgie, then opened his car door and breathed in, shaking his words.

'She's not in there love, she's in here.'

He gestured towards his heart and gave her a reassuring smile. She knew it was time to go but to never forget.

Elliot Cassley eyed up the silky smooth surface of the lake through the thinnest pebble he could find. Breathing in slowly, he gazed through his fingers then started to move his arm back and forth, building up momentum to throw it. The school trip to Brecon had been torturous for him and catching a few moments peace on his own was quite welcoming. Although he was nearing twelve years old, he was smaller than average. With thick blonde hair and a fixed brace on his teeth, which he absolutely hated the sight of. He was two weeks into a new term at a new school after his mum had decided to move him and his younger sister Alice from their old town just outside Cardiff back to Northshore, a small town where his grandparents still lived. He was dealing with a lot of heartache, missing his old friends and missing his dad. He struggled with the guilt of missing him. He had deserted them all, running off with a younger woman from work. It had been months since he had seen him, just short awkward phone calls twice a week. He exhaled out and threw the pebble as hard as he could. It skipped six times before its smaller repetitive skips finally swallowed it under the water. He knew he had ten more minutes before the teacher wanted them all back at the bus, so he kept skipping as many stones as he could, taking in the fresh air and enjoying the last of the dryer weather before winter fully took hold. Elliot smiled, he remembered his dad teaching him how to skip stones in the summer heat when they were on holiday in France two years before. He closed his eyes smiling as the happy memory came back to him, seeing once again the huge Lake Bourget and feeling his dad's hand on his shoulder.

'What you doing Toady?'

Elliot suddenly got a cold feeling on the back of his neck as he realised he wasn't alone anymore and was quickly snapped out of his happy daydream. Since starting at Northgate Comprehensive school, two of his classmates had taken it upon themselves to taunt him daily. Usually commenting on the two small warts he had on his right hand. The main thing he hated about them was the new name they had given him because of that, which unfortunately seemed to be sticking with the other students - 'Toady'.

'Find any of your slimy family in that lake Toady?'

'Yeah is that why you're down here all on your own Toady?!'

The two boys Dillon Davies and Carl Coombes both laughed at their immature repetitive jibes, knowing full well how upsetting they were being and relishing every minute of it. Elliot was scared, not just of the boys, but what they were doing. Alienating him from everyone, singling him out to be a 'weirdo', he didn't stand a chance here and he knew it. Nobody at school would sit next to him or show any interest. His old friends were all thirty miles away getting on with life and he was stuck here, in his own little prison. He stood there silent and ignored the boys, frozen in fear of retaliation and its consequences.

'Come on Carl let's get back to the bus and get the back seats, leave cry boy Toady here with all the other gross reptiles!'

'See you on the bus Toady!' Carl sneered.

Elliot wished his friends from back home were there, they would have stood up for him. Gaz Watkins the biggest of his friends would have knocked them both on the ground and force fed them worms if he was there, he knew he would have. Life was good for Elliot before his dad left and he was miserable now. He hated him, gone now were the memories of France and the hot sun, replaced by memories of his dad sitting opposite him at their old house saying he was leaving and how everyone will be happier in the long run. How dare he turn his world upside down like this! The guilt was back again, he wondered what had happened to make his dad turn his back on them. He blamed himself for his dad's decision to leave and wondered if he could have made things easier for them somehow, with better behaviour or better school reports. His mum Tracey tried to reassure him that wasn't the case, but it never helped his anxiety and he always secretly worried that he was to blame.

He looked down at his feet and kicked into the bank of the lake, all the other pupils had now started to gather, and he knew he should head back too. He dug out one last stone from the earth and cleaned off the mud with his fingers. Turning around and looking at his bullies, he had a sudden urge to throw it right at them. But he turned back to the lake and threw the best distance he'd done all day. Finally, a smile, though he knew it would be short lived after he got back on the bus.

An hour after leaving their sleepy little estate just outside Cheltenham, Georgie looked out of the sunroof of her dad's car and gazed at the huge towers and suspender cables of the Severn Bridge as they drove underneath. As they approached the toll booth, she passed over the handful of change her father had given to her in preparation.

'Thank you sweetheart, you looking forward to seeing the new house?'

'Yes and no I guess,' she said.

Thomas wound down his window and handed the change to the toll collector and waited for the barrier to raise. Georgie wondered if anyone really liked working in one of those plastic little toll boxes all day, thinking it must be quite claustrophobic for them. As the barrier raised her dad hit the accelerator. He had a nice car, a Jaguar XJS and enjoyed the power it had under the bonnet.

'I'm going to order in a takeaway tonight, we can pop out tomorrow and get some supplies in after we've visited your new school.' he said.

'Northgate, didn't you go there?'

'I did, it was the best school in the area at the time. But that was twenty five years ago, let's hope it hasn't slipped eh?!'

'Will they make fun of my accent there Dad? Grandad always used to comment on my - 'posh' accent.'

'I'm sure you'll get some attention for it, look at me I've put up with it all these years, even from your mother! You wouldn't believe how many patients called me 'boyo' or 'Taff' at the surgery. Just pretend it doesn't bother you and be confident in yourself. Anyone who has an issue with how you sound will soon lose interest if you don't rise to it.'

Georgie always loved her dad's advice, not having her mum around had meant they talked more now than they used to. She knew her dad struggled with what to say sometimes, but his level headed nature always brought out a sensible answer to things.

Elliot was relieved when he heard the hiss and squeak of the school bus door opening in front of him, he'd survived another Thursday and had only one day left until he could relax into the weekend. They had arrived back from the trip late so there was no need for him to go back into school, he could go straight home from the drop off and he couldn't wait to get out of there for some peace. As he had predicted his journey home on the bus was full of insults and verbal abuse from the bullies at the back of the bus. Of course, none of the other children stood up to them or took his side, but he could see remorse in some of the faces. Elliot's house was a ten minute walk from the school and his mum completely trusted him to navigate himself safely to and from there. He lived in a small cul-de-sac with four houses around a small roundabout. Nearby was the town's football pitch and a park with huge trees surrounding it and a gentle river running next to the houses. His mum was always in work for the first hour of him being home, she worked in the town but had to collect Alice from the local childminder. Elliot wasn't trusted to carry his door key with him at the risk of it getting lost, so his mum always hid one under the flower pot next to the front door. Northsore's crime rate was practically non-existent, however Elliot coming from the city would always check he wasn't being watched before reaching for it.

As Elliot opened the door he could hear his German shepherd Chinook barking from the kitchen, eager to see him. The kitchen door would bounce in its frame as the giant dog would lunge itself at it trying to almost break though, desperate to make a fuss of his owner. As Elliot opened the kitchen door he immediately landed flat on his back as Chinook's huge paws had landed on his chest and pushed him down. Elliot screamed with laughter as this huge black and brown beast proceeded to lick every inch of his face. If anyone was to witness this, they would have thought he was being mauled. Elliot scratched at Chinook's sides and rolled over onto his front hiding his face and giggling, playing with Chinook like he hadn't seen him in months. The dog would play along, bouncing up and down next to him until Elliot could calm him down. Chinook was only a year old, a gift from his mum after his dad left, hoping it would bring some joy back into her son's life and maybe a little protection for the household. It had certainly worked, they were solid best friends. If Elliot wasn't in school they were together and Chinook was fiercely protective of him and his sister. After struggling on a name, his mum commented on how his tail always spun so much when he saw Elliot, saying that 'he looked like he would take off like a helicopter'. From that day on he was known as Chinook. Elliot grabbed Chinook's lead off the key rack, threw on his trainers and headed out for the dog's second walk of the day.

As he walked down to the end of his driveway to open his gate, the daylight was slowly starting to fade to a red evening hue. He saw a rather elegant car slowly turning into the estate. Northshore was a small town where the average household didn't earn a huge amount of money. Posh cars were not common on the streets there. Being originally from the city Elliot was more familiar with seeing most brands of car and he recognised this as a sapphire blue Jaguar XJS. Instantly he was impressed and wondered who was inside.

Elliot closed his gate and turned around to notice the car pull up to number 56 opposite, there was already a removals van parked on the drive unloading boxes. He wondered why he hadn't noticed that as he came home, but he put it down to being keen to see Chinook. Out of the car stood a tall dark haired man wearing glasses and an unkept beard with a kind look to his face. He glanced at Elliot and smiled, then from the other side of the car, the door slowly opened. He saw her foot first as it hit the road surface from inside the foot well, white ankle high Converse trainers followed by stone washed Levi jeans with holes in the knees. A loose plain white t-shirt followed, and there she was. With Shoulder length straight red hair and probably the coolest looking girl Elliot had ever seen.

As Georgie took in the new estate and saw the front of her new house for the first time, she turned around surprised to see four eyes staring at her from across the road. Two of them belonged to the most handsome German Shepherd she'd ever seen, who tilted its head to one side as it looked at her. The other two belonged to a blonde boy who looked the same age as her, but maybe a little shorter, who suddenly didn't know where to look. Georgie had made eye contact and for some reason, he did a very awkward wave then slowly turned away, pulling his giant dog along the pavement who was busily wagging his tail and wanting to say hi.

'He looks nice, you should have said hello.' Thomas said.

'Plenty of time for that,' Georgie was intrigued to see a boy of her own age living on the same street. Back home most of her friends were a car drive away and lived down country lanes in grand country houses, usually with their own stables or swimming pool. She preferred this, it felt more grounded. Even though her dad was a doctor he was a self made man whose parents had little money, leaving Thomas to fund his own studies with grants and loans. His finances were now better than most, but class wise they were at the lower end of Georgie's school and she always felt a little out of place surrounded by such aristocracy.

The removal men brought in the last box and wished Georgie and her dad the best before closing up the van door and heading back to their base in Gloucester. Georgie watched the van drive away and then made herself busy investigating her new home. Her dad had bought the place a few weeks before and had popped down by himself to make sure it was decorated and ready for them to move in hassle free. The smell of fresh paint and new carpet filled the house, it was a new smell for Georgie as they're old house either had tiles or bare floorboards. She liked the smell and how fresh and new it made her feel. The previous owners had left their old phone attached to the wall which was a caricature of Mickey Mouse holding a yellow phone, she laughed when she noticed it as it looked so out of place.

'Thought you'd like that, so decided to keep it!' her dad smiled.

'It so uncool I love it, does it work?!'

'Oh yeah, nothing wrong with it!' he laughed.

Georgie took the yellow phone of the receiver and listened to the dial tone giggling to herself. She couldn't wait to use it. She walked into the kitchen where her dad was unpacking and looked out the back garden. She was disappointed to see no grass, but a collection of pink and white paving slabs. The garden in the old house held precious memories of her mother. They had an old oak tree that housed a handmade swing where she'd sit on her mother's lap and gently swing, singing songs to each other. But this was more practical, she knew her dad wasn't into gardening and the less maintenance he had to deal with around the house the better. She thought at least a basketball hoop wouldn't go amiss out there, the slabs would be perfect for dribbling a ball back and forth with her dad on the weekends.

'Georgie, why don't you go for a walk and check out the park? It'll be dark in about half an hour. Go and get your bearings a bit, I'm okay here unpacking. just follow the lane that runs behind the house.'

Georgie didn't need telling twice, as much as she wanted to stay with her dad she couldn't wait to check out the fields, especially on her bike. She'd never had such expansive greenery so close to home before, it was exciting and she couldn't wait to make great use of it.

Elliot had been walking around the park throwing Chinook's ball for him, intrigued by his new neighbours. He couldn't get the image of the girl out of his head and wondered, what was her story? Why had she moved to Northshore? Had her parents separated too? Were they escaping to a new life? Where was her mum? As he was throwing the ball across the expanse of the football pitch he pondered what he would say to her first if she spoke to him and how he'd manage to introduce himself. He thought that he needed to make an effort to try and make at least one new friend in this town. He'd failed to connect with anyone at Northgate School so far, even with the help of the teachers trying to pair him with 'similar' boys at school, he found it difficult to engage with any of the kids there. He threw the ball hard and far for Chinook and laughed as the dog went bounding as fast as he could across the pitch, nearly going over his head as he tried to grab the ball in his mouth while still running.

'I'll just play it cool,' he said to himself out loud, when out of nowhere came a voice.

'Hi I'm Georgie, Georgie Rivers.'

Elliot nearly jumped out of his skin as he realised he wasn't alone.

'Uh hi, hi there I'm an idiot ... I mean, I'm Elliot!'

Elliot calling himself an idiot internally seemed to end up being vocalised out of confusion and he quickly had to correct himself. Georgie laughed but quickly replied.

'So what is it, Elliot or Idiot?'

'Elliot, it's definitely Elliot, I'm sorry I was in a world of my own. Nice to meet you.'

'Just playing it cool there I gather?' she replied.

Elliot and Georgie laughed in agreement and he called Chinook back with a loud whistle, the giant dog came racing back towards them and greeted Georgie with an excited nudge of his wet nose on her hand, asking for a fuss.

'This is Chinook, don't let him scare you, he's a big old softie just a little nuts.'

Georgie made a fuss of Chinook and Elliot saw instantly that his dog approved. They started to walk across the pitch and Elliot decided to give Georgie a little description of what was around her. He had already extensively investigated his surroundings when he first moved there. He had already found the river that led all the way to the school, then eventually to the estuary that opened out to the cliffs and the ocean. Georgie had lots of questions about the school and Elliot tried to be positive for her even though he hated it there. He was honest about the bullies but told her to make her own opinion of the place. He didn't want to come across as desperate or influence her decisions for his benefit. Mainly, he wanted to see if he wasn't the only one that thought the place was difficult to handle.

When they arrived back at the estate, Elliot's mum Tracey and his sister Alice were chatting to Thomas on the street, exchanging greetings and introductions. For the first time Georgie noticed her father had a brightness, almost shy look about him which was strange. Georgie and Elliot looked at each other and rolled their eyes simultaneously.

CHAPTER TWO
FAMILY SECRET

Georgie was awoken by the piercing noise of her alarm clock, the hammer furiously bouncing between the two bells. The clock was so loud she wondered if the entire town had heard it. She suddenly felt a little awkward knowing she was waking for the first time in a new town. She reached over and put her finger in between the hammer and the bells to stop the ringing before turning the lever to disarm it. She glanced at the clock, it read eight o'clock and she turned to look at the window. As organised as Thomas Rivers had been with getting the house ready for them there was one essential home comfort he had overlooked, curtains. Georgie smiled, stretched out and put her feet on the floor scrunching up her toes over the new carpet underneath. The carpet was already something she preferred to the cold floorboards of the old house.

As Georgie arrived at the bottom of the stairs, she could hear her dad busy in the kitchen making them breakfast. Stacked on the floor by the front door was her father's collection of old climbing magazines. Thomas had been keen to get some quality time spent with Georgie on the weekends, just the two of them. He decided to introduce her to his favourite pastime, which had eluded him in recent years, rock climbing. He had been a keen rock climber in his university days and always liked the discipline that it allowed him to switch off from day to day life and focus his concentration on the climb and nothing else. Georgie had loved it from the very first session. The feel of the rope, the technicality of using the belays and carabiners to secure her weight to assist her climb and descent. Thomas fed off Georgie's enthusiasm for the sport and was thrilled to finally have a common interest and activity they could share together. Georgie had become a strong climber and her dad soon gave her a taste of the real thing on day trips to the Peak District. On their journey to Wales from England, he had promised Georgie a trip to the Brecon Beacons once they had settled in at Northshore.

'Don't expect this every morning but seen as it's our first day here I thought I'd make pancakes.' Thomas said smiling.

Georgie felt spoilt, she loved having pancakes for breakfast but since her mum died her dad had only managed a bare basic breakfast for them in the mornings and that was normally on the weekends when life was a little quieter. Georgie was usually first up, so she had the duty of throwing some cereal in a bowl or trying to do toast for them both, which she normally managed to burn. But her dad appreciated it and a quick scrape in the sink usually made it edible.

Thomas stacked the pancakes on a plate and placed them in the middle of the table as Georgie sat down. To her surprise he'd even poured her a glass of orange juice and made them both a cup of tea.

'I'm looking forward to getting back into climbing soon dad, how far away is Brecon from here?'

'Oh, a little over an hour, not far really. I unpacked all our equipment and hung it up in the garage, just need to find a home for all of those magazines. I may take them to the surgery and donate them to the waiting room table.'

Thomas poured himself a glass of orange juice from the bottle and started to pour raisins and blueberries over his first pancake, Georgie sensed he was feeling happier. Their new surroundings were having a positive effect on them both, not having a constant reminder of her mum and her illness was a great weight off their shoulders. Since being at the new house Georgie realised her memories seemed to be of more happier times with her mum, rather than the ghostly reminders of the hospital equipment from her bed room.

'So, we've got a busy day today love, we're popping to Northgate at nine thirty for the quick meet and greet with the head, then I have to go and sign a few forms and show my face at the new surgery.'

'How long will that take?'

'I can't see it taking longer than half an hour at the school, maybe an hour at the surgery? I should probably measure up for some curtains then!' Thomas said promisingly as he fed himself a huge mouthful of his rolled-up pancake.

Georgie was keen to investigate her new town further and hoped her dad would let her wander through the town while he was busy at the surgery. He'd been a little overprotective of her the last few months, but he was slowly letting her venture off on her own, so long as she didn't go too far. Moving to a house that had a park nearby was a big influence in his decision to move to the estate. Georgie would have her freedom to explore while being safe from the hustle and bustle of a busy town and he could take baby steps in letting her go out on her own, for his sake more than hers. When her mum was alive he was always first to admit that he let her do all the safeguarding when it came to Georgie's whereabouts. Georgie was more than aware of this and was happy to make things easy for him by not pushing her luck. She tended not to stay out too long with her friends back home, she knew he worried, and it was the last thing he needed. But Georgie was curious by nature and loved to investigate. Being in a new town, she was curious to get out and start exploring, especially that she now lived so close to the coast. She'd only visited the coast a handful of times and now it was on her doorstep.

A few miles away in an industrial unit on the outskirts of Northshore, a run down body shop had been rented temporarily much to the landlords satisfaction. When a new franchise repair garage had opened in the town, the tenant of the unit had struggled to keep up his payments and the landlord was left with an empty building. After being vacant for nearly fourteen months he was happy to have had an offer of six months rent up front, in cash. He didn't bother questioning the estate agent on what the tenant wanted the building for, as far as he was concerned it was insured and he was back making a profit from it. So long as they didn't burn the place down he had little concerns for how they intended to use it. The building was empty but still had the sign 'Best Auto Repair' above the huge roller shutter door and a worn poster on the customer entrance emblazoned with the slogan 'We make friends by accident!'. The building still smelled of body filler and spray paint with the faint whiff of what was once a thriving business.

Madeline Wolf sat upstairs inside the old unit at a desk studying black and white photographs spread out all over her makeshift desk. Dominik Carver and Dutch both sat opposite watching as she carefully studied each one with a magnifying glass. Dominik's foot was in a full plaster cast and he cursed as he used a long ruler to scratch down inside it. Dutch was busy rolling a coin through his fingers and chewing on a wooden lollipop stick, examining Madeline Wolf as she carefully inspected the many photographs.

'You say this second entrance is at least thirty feet high?' Madeline said.

'Easily,' Dominik replied sucking air through his teeth as he scratched at his injured leg.

Dutch leaned forward to stand up, putting the coin into his jacket pocket, he walked over to stand next to Madeline tossing the lollipop stick on the floor. Leaning over her he gathered up three of the photos and started to point at specific areas of the prints, moving Madeline's hand with the magnifying glass to direct her. As he was giving her valuable information she tolerated his patronising action.

'The entrance is just shy of thirty feet from the cave floor, high above this larger door here. It is approximately the size of a small bathroom window, maybe half a meter wide and even less in height. No regular sized adult is going to fit through that hole they made, I'm sure of that. The mortar they used that surrounds it makes it impossible to dig it larger without causing it to crumble and collapse, which would completely ruin our chances of opening the main entrance below. Well, unless we resort to dynamite blasting, but that'll attract unwanted attention and possibly destroy what's behind.'

Dominik threw down the ruler in frustration, cursing again in French under his breath and hobbled across to a serving trolley. He poured three cups of black coffee from a cafetiere, dropped one sugar cube into each cup, then placed them on the desk. Dutch and Madeline stopped their discussion to observe Dominik and his mild rant, then concentrated their attention back to the prints.

Dominik reached over and slid a photograph toward Madeline, showing him standing next to an opening for scale. Recessed into the cave wall appeared to be a man-made door about a meter in height that had no obvious handles or locks and looked impossible to open.

'As your map suggests Madame, we have to enter via the opening high up where your cross symbol is located here.' Dominik tapped on one of the photographs before continuing to speak, 'Then we believe we can gain access to open this larger door from behind. I did attempt to climb up to get a closer look but that's where my climbing skills failed, and I plummeted to the cave floor. If our friend Dutch here didn't carry me out, I probably would have died.'

Dominik slumped back down into his chair with his coffee, causing months of dust to flurry around him. Dutch wandered over to the window that was being half draped by an old dust sheet. He pulled it down to allow more light into the dusty office.

'Ms Wolf, I must say from my experience that the door looks a lot older than we were expecting it to,' he said, as he turned back to look at them, 'It predates the end of the War, I'd put a thousand dollars on it. But I think you already know that?'

Madeline leaned back into her chair and stared at Dominik, tapping her fingers on the desk considering her options. Madeline had the power to stare through a person as though she was invading their very soul. She then stood up and walked across to her briefcase sitting at the bottom of an old wooden coat stand in the corner of the room. She opened the leather briefcase and pulled out an old journal, barely managing to keep itself in one piece being held together by numerous elastic bands.

'My aunt discovered this journal a few years ago when she had one of her many portrait frames repaired. They were her fathers during World War Two and had been hidden and moved so often they needed some attention. She was slowly getting them professionally refurbished. The painting in question had been handed down for generations. The framer thankfully was a family friend and an honest man who alerted her to his discovery immediately. He was right to do so, he was paid well for his discretion. The journal was concealed along with the map and had been there for over a hundred years. The documents predate the painting and how they got there neither my aunt or I have any clue.' Madeline carefully removed the elastic bands as she walked back towards the desk.

'Inside this journal are the notes of my fifth great grandfather Klaus Von Jürgen Wolfgang. Which through extensive genealogy we managed to clarify. Although, we noticed he did change his surname from Wolfgang to simply Wolf before marrying, we're assuming for anonymities sake.' Madeline handed the delicate papers to Dominik and sat back in her chair.

Dominik looked intriguingly through the antique documents. Though the print was heavily faded and barely legible, he managed to pick out basic German words that he could recognise; Höhle meaning cave, Juwelen which was easily picked out as jewels and gefangen, he translated to the best of his knowledge as captured or trapped.

'Madame these papers are barely legible. What help is this to us?' Dominik said indignantly.

Madeline reached inside her left jacket pocket and revealed new folded papers. She unfolded them and laid them out on the desk amongst the black and white photographs.

'I tracked down a lab in Prague that managed to extract the writing using UV light. They then photographed the pages for me, I have them here and as you can see it was quite successful.' Madeline turned the pages towards Dutch and Dominik who both came forward to inspect them more closely.

Dominik's languages were varied being fluent in English, Spanish and his native French. Dutch coming from Philadelphia, USA hadn't excelled academically, signing up for the marines as soon as he graduated from high school. Both the men struggled to make sense of the German document laid out in front of them. Madeline Wolf took in a deep breath and began to take them through her ancestors notes.

'These notes detail the story of Klaus Von Jürgen Wolfgang. He was - I am led to believe from reading this journal, a pirate.' Madeline stared at the men awaiting a reaction. Dominik smirked while letting out a sniff of air and shook his head in disbelief, which made Dutch glance at him in frustration. He wanted to hear what Madeline had to say and Dominik stifled his reaction. Both the men returned their attention to her and Madeline continued to talk.

'There's no written date present, but our analysis has carbon dated the ink to around 1740 to 1760. We can't get any more accurate than that unfortunately, but it does tie in with his age on his death certificate. Reading the journal, I found it hard to believe also, but now we've found this cave it appears we may be onto something. The notes in the journal detail everything, it's all here in faded black and white.' Standing at the front of the desk Madeline slowly made her way back around to her seat continuing to talk.

'Klaus was once a first mate for a pirate known by the name John Kelly. Kelly's crew had grown tired of his leadership and had a vote of no confidence in their captain. They abandoned him in a port in southern Spain stealing his ship The Dragon's Eye in the process. The ship was said to be one of the most beautiful yet dangerous ships of its time. It was stolen from the British and was originally known as the HMS Prince George. It was thought to be destroyed by a fire in official documents, but this was a cover up at the time. The British didn't want anyone discovering it had been commandeered by pirates to avoid the embarrassment. Later it was heavily modified with 36 pounder long gun cannons and fixed large scale harpoons. Once Klaus had replaced Kelly they set sail for East Africa, he had been told of great riches coming out of Egypt and they wanted to find their fortune there before returning home to Germany.'

Madeline sat back down keeping her eyes fixed on the men. Madeline was secretly in doubt as to how they were going to react to her story, she considered stopping but seeing she had their full attention, she continued with her story.

'En route, Klaus' ship the Dragon's Eye became involved in a battle between a rival pirate ship known as The Good Grief, along the south coast of Africa. Klaus and his men managed to overpower them and boarded the ship to find riches far beyond their imagination. Klaus gave the men of The Grief an ultimatum, they either joined him or went down with their ship. It's written that two of the men pledged allegiance to Klaus and true to his word, he set fire to the ship's rum stores with the remaining men still aboard and watched it sink.'

Dominik interrupted, 'So a relative of yours was a cold-blooded mass murderer Madame? Explains a lot!' His laugh was high and shrill, Madeline stared coldly at

Dominik not giving him the pleasure of entertaining his humour. Dutch had listened carefully to her every word and was eager to know more.

'Sorry Ms Wolf, but what does this old pirate story have to do with a cave in South Wales of all places? We were under the impression you wanted us to find lost artefacts taken from Berlin?' he asked turning to look at Dominik expecting validation. Madeline nodded and looked down at the reprint of Klaus' journal, she turned to the last page and replied.

'The Dragon's Eye never reached Egypt. Klaus turned the ship around and set a course for home. Little did Klaus know that the two men he acquired from The Grief were planning their revenge. Klaus' plan was to drop anchor outside Germany and to dock in Hamburg from a smaller vessel to avoid inspection and also suspicion. The English Channel was obviously heavily guarded by the Royal Navy at this time, so Klaus opted to pass through the Celtic Sea, then up between Ireland and Wales thinking it would save them time. It was here that the two men sabotaged the ship by setting alight to the gunpowder stores. By the time the crew realised what had happened it was too late, the men were gone. Presumably, they jumped overboard with the ship engulfed in flames. However, the last page of Klaus' journal indicates they managed to escape the ship on lifeboats, with most of the treasures in hand.' Madeline slowly turned the pages in front of her, she knew them off by heart but felt that she needed something to focus on.

'Klaus and two of his crew were marooned in Wales, as it now appears here in Northshore for around two months according to the journal. It would have been impossible to travel through Britain at the time carrying all their hoard on horseback. So they stashed most of it in a cave, carrying only a little and left the family cross of Klaus Wolfgang as a marker to return in the future to retrieve it by sea. But for reasons unknown, he never did come back.'

Dominik laughed out loud and clapped his hands together, he stood up as best he could dragging his injured leg across the room toward the window.

'You're expecting us to believe that Ma Chérie? The idea of pirates is a little difficult to swallow these days no? Stolen paintings hidden by U-boat officers during World War Two, that was a lot easier to believe... but this, I'm not so sure'.

Just then the room was filled with a loud buzzing noise, someone was at the main door ringing the doorbell.

Outside stood next to his Austin Maestro 500 van, Simon Jenkins had arrived to give his new tenants the keys to the roller shutter door. He was busy admiring the brand new Land Rover Defender parked outside and was wondering to himself what sort of business his new tenants were bringing into the town. Clearly, they had a few quid already he thought to himself. He heard the door unlock and open behind him and he turned around to be greeted by the largest man he'd ever laid eyes on. Dutch stepped out closing the door behind him and approached Simon holding his hand out to shake.

'You must be our new landlord?' he said confidently.

In his surprise at the sheer size of the man in front of him, Simon got flustered and the first words out of his mouth were confusing even for him.

'Am I? I am … yes. How do you know that?' he said, Simon gave off the air that he was a successful man by accident rather than intelligence.

Dutch pointed at Simon's van which had 'Jenkins Properties and Hire' written on the side of it. He had inherited his father's estate which included ownership of many of the local business buildings and surrounding land when he had died. Simon never saw eye to eye with his estranged father and knew he was always considered a failure by who was once the town's most successful businessman. Simon merged his small tool hire business and property development firms together under the one brand, mainly as one last little dig to the deceased patriarch who would have hated the idea of his heritage being cheapened. There hadn't been much property development since Simon had taken over, but the properties he did own were still doing well.

'I have the keys for the shutter doors here for you, they unlock from inside if I remember, simply a padlock and then pull down on the chains. I'm happy to show you if you like?'

Simon gestured to enter the building, but Dutch stood firmly in front of him holding out his hand.

'That won't be necessary Sir but thank you for dropping them around. Have a nice day.'

Dutch replied politely but short and to the point. He nodded at Simon and returned into the building locking the door behind him. Simon seemed a little perplexed by the man's eagerness to return inside and was annoyed with himself for not asking what they planned to use the unit for. Not that he really cared, he had his money and he was merely being nosey. It all seemed a little strange to him, rent paid up in full, an expensive Land Rover and an American who looked like he could snap an average sized man in two. As Simon climbed into his van to return back to his hire shop, he was unaware that he was being studied from the window above.

'What did he want?' demanded Madeline Wolf as Dutch returned to the office up the stairs.

Dutch threw the small cluster of keys on the desk and sat back down.

'He's our new landlord and was dropping off these for the roller shutter doors. I guess he forgot to hand them over to the estate agent we dealt with? Shame I've already cut off the lock they belong to and replaced it with one of my own,' he said sarcastically. 'I don't think we'll see him again.'

Dominik was staring out of the window at the coastline, visible from the unit. He was still holding the original journal papers in his hand, feeling the soft paper between his fingers. Dominik needed this job, he had defaulted on his mortgage due to his gambling in the Paris casinos and owed a lot of unfavourable men a lot of money. Madeline was paying them well with the promise of a bonus if the artefacts they recovered were found to be lucrative. What did it matter if they were paintings stolen by the Nazi's years before or jewels stolen by a so-called pirate, centuries before? He had no choice he had to go with it. But he had seen the cave, he had seen the risks and the problems they faced.

'Madame your story is fascinating, a little difficult to believe but I'll reserve judgement until we see what's behind that door. So long as my ankle allows me I'm still on board. No pun intended.' Dominik lifted his coffee cup up in a display of cheers and took a long noisy gulp.

'The problem is getting through the door,' Dutch spoke up and turned facing them both.

'I know people were smaller in the old days but one of Klaus' shipmates must have been either a boy or a dwarf, you know ... uh, a little person.' Dominik and Madeline stared at Dutch waiting for him to get to his point.

'What I'm saying is, we'll need someone small too. Plus getting all the gear and equipment in there, it ain't gonna be easy.' Dutch ran his hands through his hair and looked up at the ceiling as if looking for his next words.

'Realistically it's going to take a few trips. I can get a small ladder in there to insert climbing bolts to the wall up to a point. But I'm too large to climb high up between the wall and the cave ceiling, especially with all those stalactites. We're still left with the small problem of finding someone ... small enough.' Dutch looked at Madeline hoping for an answer.

Madeline already had a plan in motion, she was a calculating and cold woman. Born and bred into a cold war soviet run East Berlin, she had no attachment or emotion towards anyone in the west. Madeline would attempt anything to get where she wanted or get what she desired. People were expendable to her, even age was of no significance, in fact she had an instant hatred for anyone under the age of twenty five. She wanted nothing more than to gain entrance to the cave and to retrieve what her ancestor had left for her, so she could have more, so she could be the richest and most powerful woman, whatever the cost. Madeline opened the drawer of her desk and pulled out a bottle of Himbeergiest, a raspberry German schnapps and poured a healthy serving into an empty tumbler on the desk. She took a large swig and enjoyed the sweet strong burn from the alcohol as it descended down her throat. After admiring the aftertaste for a brief second, she finished the rest of the drink placing the glass down hard on the desk. Dutch and Dominik both waited in anticipation of what she would say next, after all she was in charge of this expedition. When she simply said.

'Isn't there a school nearby?'.

CHAPTER THREE
NORTHGATE

The gates to Northgate school must have been repainted a hundred times, yet the corroded wrought iron still ate and bubbled through the royal blue paint. They stood tall with the school's shield pride of place at the centre. Separated into quarters, the insignia featured an anvil, a ship, three chevrons and a red dragon. Georgie wondered what they all represented, the dragon and the ship being the only obvious symbols for the coastal town of Northshore, being located in South Wales. Northgate was an old school, a glorious red brick monument that was originally constructed with the sole purpose of becoming a grammar school for the few hundred children who successfully passed their eleven plus exam in the late forties. The government's education system soon turned the building into a comprehensive school during the early seventies and filled its classes with children from three neighbouring towns. It now catered for a thousand pupils and as the prospectus that Georgie had received in the post weeks before stated, was 'home to the best under sixteen rugby and hockey teams in South Wales… for the last four years in a row'. As Georgie stood out of her dad's car she noticed the red brick facade fed back into what looked like a grey almost temporary looking extension twice the size of the old grammar school. The old school couldn't cope with the escalating needs of the towns' children and it had to expand as quickly and as cheaply as the local council could afford. With flat felt covered roofs, dirty aluminium windows and stained rendered walls. The more modern building had suffered years of pupil abuse. The walls were now decorated with crude graffiti and it certainly brought shame on the glory of the earlier architecture standing proud at the front. As grand as the old school looked from the front, the extension to its rear was looking tired and in desperate need of rejuvenation.

Georgie felt uneasy seeing this, she had been fortunate to have spent her education up to now in a far better school environment. She thought back to the school she had left behind, with its ornate hanging baskets and ivy crawling over most of the walls. Her school was built during the regency period and was located between Gloucester and Cheltenham. She always felt that the building had an identity of its own and always enjoyed the welcoming view of the stone pillars as she walked into school in the morning. At break times, her school yard stretched out into acres of greenery which was always a welcome energy boost for her between lessons. Looking at Northgate, she found it hard to imagine finding any motivation to go there every day and felt sympathy towards the pupils. It was grey and drab, with a tarmac covered schoolyard with faded white lines of what looked like a netball pitch.

From an upstairs classroom window, Elliot watched his new neighbours car arrive in through the gates and he couldn't help but feel nervous. He had instantly taken a liking to Georgie and couldn't wait to spend some more time getting to know her once the school day was over. He had agreed to meet her at four o'clock to take her for a quick trip around the town on their bikes. He knew the light would fade quickly, but he was confident he'd get an hour in before they had to get back home. He was impressed the night before when he noticed leaning on her garage wall, the same Raleigh BMX Burner he had, and he hoped Georgie rode as well as he did. One escape for Elliot in Northshore was taking his BMX down to the old industrial estate where he would use the piled-up gravel and machinery as makeshift ramps and jumps. Aggressively taking his frustrations out on his bike from the days torment at school. An hour of adrenaline fuelled riding including near miss accidents was always a boost for his self-esteem, even if his heart was in his mouth most of the time and his wrists ached from landing too hard on his front wheel. Thankfully he always knew he had Chinook there to raise the alarm back at his house if he ever hurt himself too severely, but thankfully he'd avoided any 'Lassie' moments as his mum called it.

'Mr Cassley are you still with us?!'

Mr Cleverly was head of maths and a veteran at Northgate. He stood tall with a bald head and eyes that were slightly crossed. No one was ever quite sure if he was looking at them or something else just to their left. He took no nonsense and didn't suffer fools gladly that was certain, but he always rewarded pupils with praise and respect if they had earned it. Despite his strict disposition he was a very good teacher.

'Yes sir, sorry' Elliot replied.

As he sat back down, he noticed all the eyes of the classroom were focussed on him. A few sniggers and whispers made him feel exposed and he was annoyed with himself for attracting unwanted attention. After he endured a few seconds of glaring pupils, they turned their heads toward the teacher who was explaining Pythagoras' theorem on the blackboard for the fifth time that week. Two tables across and in front, were Dillon Davies and Carl Coombes. Both of the boys were still turned and facing Elliot smirking. He decided to stare back at them, he was growing tired of their bullying and he noticed Carl whisper into Dillon's ear, Dillon reacted with a big grin and nodded his head in appreciation. Elliot knew they were talking about him and his blood started to boil. Something about meeting Georgie the day before had boosted his confidence. He didn't feel so alone in this little town anymore.

Georgie sat in the Headmistress' office and stared at Ms Verita James' enormous hair. She couldn't quite figure out if it was natural or a wig, it was so thick and jet black and her thick glasses seemed to be engulfed either side of her face by it. The office had an overpowering smell of potpourri and Georgie wondered what smell Ms James was trying to disguise with it, she considered that maybe she had birds nesting in her hair and tried desperately not to laugh at her own joke. Along the top row of a large cabinet were dozens of hockey trophies, and below that there were wooden shield plaques which the school had been awarded for various rugby and football tournaments over the years.

'How is your active lifestyle Georgie, do you partake in any sports?'

Ms James had a very low voice, Georgie was almost sure she must get mistaken for a man over the telephone.

'I enjoy rock climbing and riding my BMX mainly, but I also played lacrosse at my last school.'

Ms James scoffed at Georgie's response and clapped her hands together.

'Rock climbing and lacrosse?! Well there won't be any exotic sports here at Northgate young lady, here us girls play hockey. I coach the sixth form, real strong girls we have this year. I'm sure you'll get the hang of it, it's like lacrosse in many ways only a bit more civilised.'

Georgie glanced at her father and rolled her eyes, he smiled with an expression of a mild apology and she knew he was understanding her internal disgust. Ms James leapt out of her chair and standing in her doorway called across the hall to the office opposite.

'Mrs Price, where would I find class 2E at this precise moment?' she smiled while staring into silent space awaiting a call back from her secretary. There was the sound of an office chair rolling across the hardwood floor. The ruffle of papers and then a croaky older voice called out after clearing her throat with a very chesty cough.

'Mathematics - Mr Cleverly, Room 4'

'Perfect, come on then Mr and Miss Rivers, let's give you a tour of the lower school and we'll finish with a quick introduction to your class with Mr Cleverly. Not only is he your maths teacher but also your form tutor, two birds with one stone and all that!' Ms James snorted.

Georgie felt Northgate had a strange odour to it. Walking around the corridors and being shown the gym hall, then the assembly hall, she noticed there was a strong dusty dry scent of wood for the most part. Probably due to the old radiators and pipework that laced the huge rooms and corridors. They were scorching hot to get the large building anywhere near warm. Earlier, Georgie had placed her hand on top of one of the cast iron radiators, enticed by its rounded top that looked like it needed to be touched to be appreciated. She had quickly pulled her hand back due to the heat, promising herself to avoid doing that again anytime soon. The school also had a faint sickly whiff of bubble gum to it and Georgie wondered how many students had hidden their used gum under the windowsills that lined the hallways outside the classrooms. As Georgie walked around the atrium centre of the school behind Ms James and her father who were discussing exam results and old teachers that her dad remembered, she peered into the classrooms watching the students being taught. The students also noticed Georgie, she made eye contact with some of them, which left her feeling very much like the new girl. Looking at the boys and the girls dressed in their black and grey uniforms, she wondered if they enjoyed it at Northgate and which if any, she'd be friends with. Some of the children smiled, others looked blankly at her. The occasional few, as she'd predicted pulled a face. Both the humorous and vicious types, reminding her that even though she was one, kids could be cruel. Georgie paid no attention to bullies and they rarely bothered her, she had a knack of switching off from it thanks to her father's advice and normally had quick wits to outsmart the typical school bully.

As they reached the top of the stairs, Ms James announced in her booming low voice that they were approaching the art classes before leading to their final destination of the maths block. Georgie feeling a little downbeat by the lacklustre appearance of Northgate and the idea of playing hockey for the next four years was dragging her feet up the stairs. As she peered up, she was greeted by a huge colourful mural of what she instantly recognised as Roy Lichtenstein's famous painting 'Whaam!'. The 1963 pop art piece was one of her favourites after doing a module on the movement at her old school the year before, including Lichtenstein and the likes of Andy Warhol in sixties America. Georgie's eyes widened as she took in the simple but powerful action from the comic strip art, replicated in front of her. The fighter jet looking like it was flying faster than speed itself, shooting missiles at its enemy plane causing it to explode in bright red and yellow flames with the huge WHAAM! text emblazoned above it. Georgie stopped and took in the painting that had obviously been completed by the students and thought to herself 'Maybe it's not all bad here.' As she looked down she noticed a female teacher was looking at her through the open door with a warm smile. The inside of the class was colourful and warm with paintings and artwork covering the grey lifeless walls, she noticed the radio was on. Maybe amongst this drab institution there was a small hint of life and inspiration to be had. Georgie smiled back at the teacher and hurried to catch up with her tour guide.

Georgie's dad and Ms James were already standing outside of room 4's door, Ms James primed with a knock to open and enter with the authority that a Headmistress demands. Elliot was eager for the class to see his new friend but found himself feeling anxious that he was sat alone. He started to question whether Georgie would notice him, or worse, notice that he clearly wasn't one of the cool kids. His relationship with Georgie was too new for him to know what direction it would take, and he was worried she'd prefer one of the more popular groups in the class. Mr Cleverly happily accepted the interruption as he could tell he wasn't getting anywhere with the class that morning. He signalled for the class to stand as Ms James entered the room, allowing her to grant them permission back into their seats.

Thomas and Georgie both waited at the door before Georgie was ushered into the classroom.

'Thank you Mr Cleverly. Class 2E we have a wonderful new pupil joining us as of next week. Georgie come on in.'

Thomas stayed in the hallway not wanting to embarrass his daughter in front of her peers. Georgie raised her eyebrows towards her dad as if to say, 'wish me luck' and strolled in to stand beside Ms James. Feeling a little examined. Georgie stood at the front of the class taking in the faces of her soon to be classmates. She could tell she was being brutally analysed by the table of 'pretty girls' and noticed a table of boys laughing quietly to each other, however she kept a pleasant smile on her face and tried not to look fazed. Through all the new faces she fixed on Elliot at the back, sat alone but upright with a huge smile on his face. Seeing Elliot meant a lot and put Georgie at ease, she couldn't understand why everyone avoided him and suspected nobody had even given him a chance.

'Georgie is joining us from Cheltenham everybody, so please give her a warm welcome as I'm sure coming to Northgate is a big move for her. Mr Cleverly can we leave Georgie with you for a few minutes while we sort out some administration paperwork in the office. Give her a ten-minute taste of your excellent teachings?!'

'Of course, welcome to the school Georgie, please find a seat somewhere.'

Mr Cleverly gestured to the class, there were a couple of empty seats towards the front, but Georgie already knew where she wanted to sit. She took a quick glance at her dad as Ms James closed the door and she gave a shy wave as she watched them walk back down the corridor through the class window. She looked back into the classroom and at Mr Cleverly, gave him an acknowledging nod and started to walk towards the back of the class to sit next to Elliot.

Elliot was so excited and relieved Georgie had sat next to him. The whole class was turned once again staring at him but this time he wasn't alone and this time he didn't care that everyone was looking at him, he was only interested in the new girl.

'Okay Class eyes forward.' Mr Cleverly stood for a moment, waiting for everyone to turn their attention back to him.

'Georgie we're looking at Pythagoras' theorem this week. I've just set the class a task of five equations from their textbooks. Elliot please lend Georgie a pen, here's a blank sheet of paper pass it back to Georgie please.'

Mr Cleverly handed a sheet of paper to the front table and the pupils passed it back from table to table to Georgie. He sat down and started marking some of the exercise books on his desk, allowing the class to quietly tackle their task at hand.

'Hey how's the tour going?' Elliot asked in a whisper.

'Fine… I kind of feel a little like an alien here, everyone seems to stare, especially the girls. We still on for the bike ride later? Think I'm going to need it.'

'Definitely, here's a pen we're on page twenty five I've already done the first two if you want to copy?'.

A few minutes past and Elliot could tell Dillon and Carl were up to something, they kept looking over at him and Georgie, chuckling to each other. Elliot was angry he didn't want these two idiots causing problems for Georgie, he'd had enough too and wanted it to stop. Out of nowhere a boy's voice shouted the word 'Ginge!'.

The class erupted into laughter and Mr Cleverly stood up and quickly had the class under control. Elliot was enraged, he knew it was Carl and he glared at the boys. As good a teacher that he was, Mr Cleverly had a handicap of being totally deaf in one ear. So even though he heard and was aware something had been shouted out, he had no clue what word it was or what direction it came from.

'Calm down you lot, Dillon, Carl I'm looking at you. No more nonsense or you're outside.' he sat back down, staring down the class before returning to his marking, he knew who the trouble was regardless of his handicap.

Georgie felt a cold shudder down her back and felt heavy in her chest, like someone had just punched her. This wasn't the first time she had been teased for her red hair and it wouldn't be the last, what she feared the most was the response from the rest of the class. Were they really all the same age she thought? Elliot had pre-warned her of the level of immaturity at the school, but she hadn't quite anticipated getting a taste of the mob mentality there quite so soon.

'It was them, they can't help themselves. They think they're so much better than everyone else and always get away with it.' Elliot whispered to Georgie, she could sense his frustration and noticed Carl and Dillon laughing and turning their heads to look at them.

'Don't worry about it, I've had worse. I've got pretty thick skin.'

'It's not the point.' Elliot turned and looked at Mr Cleverley's collection of maths books on the bookshelf next to him, there was one hardback book called 'Stoddard's New Intellectual Arithmetic'. The idea was already in his mind. Looking over at Dillon and Carl, Elliot knew they'd try something to get a rise out of the class again, he reached over and silently slid the heavy book off the shelf. Georgie watched what he was doing and shook her head in disapproval, but Elliot simply smiled and gave Georgie a wink. He pulled out an elastic band from his pencil case and wrapped it around the book holding the covers and pages firmly shut. Dillon and Carl didn't keep them waiting and sure enough they delivered another taunt.

Dillon bellowed 'Ginger nut!' at the top of his voice, drawing out the word ginger shouting it like a football chant. No sooner had he finished shouting, Elliot had quickly grabbed the old maths book off the table and launched it at Dillon's head like a frisbee. It hit Dillon square in the mouth and propelled his head backwards into Carl's face, cracking him on his nose causing it to bleed explosively. Everyone in the class witnessed what Elliot had done and burst into rapturous applause and laughter. Dillon's mouth now started to bleed, and he noticed he had chipped his front tooth. Carl started to cry in pain and clutched at his nose.

Georgie looked at Elliot and simply said 'Wham!', she didn't expect life to imitate art as closely as the painting she'd admired minutes before. Mr Cleverly bolted upright amongst the pandemonium and called for quiet in the class.

'What on earth is going on with you two?! Outside right now!' he bellowed.

'Sir! Elliot threw something at us sir!' Dillon protested spitting blood all over his desk.

'Enough rubbish from you two get outside.'

Elliot swallowed hard thinking he was in big trouble, he hadn't quite meant for the book to be so precise or do as much damage and Georgie could see his legs shaking. Mr Cleverly walked over to the bullies' desk and looked around it. Thankfully for Elliot the book he threw fell into Dillon's open bag concealing the evidence.

'What are they talking about Elliot?' Mr Cleverly was staring straight at Elliot although it looked like he was staring outside because of his wonky eyes. 'Did you throw something?'.

Elliot was silent, still in slight shock from what had just happened. Georgie had noticed the boys had football stickers on their desk when she walked past and quickly interjected.

'Mr Cleverly, I saw them squabbling over those football stickers, it looked to me like they slipped and hit each other by accident?'

Mr Cleverly looked down at the desk and sure enough saw football stickers and no book, other than the ones they had been using. He exhaled a long breath and went over to the door, walked out and closed it behind him. Georgie and Elliot sat there once again with the entire class staring at them, outside Mr Cleverly was very vocally chastising the two boys.

'Well, that showed them' Georgie said 'Can I suggest you don't hang about after school though El? They may try and jump you.' Mr Cleverly opened the door and everyone could hear the tail end of his tirade ordering the boys to the toilet to tidy themselves up.

As Mr Cleverly came back into the class, Ms James arrived swiftly behind him.

'Those two playing up again Mr Cleverly?! Send them my way next time would you? Georgie you are released for today. I hope you enjoyed your little taster at

Northgate, don't let those twits put you off. Your dad's waiting downstairs for you, I've recommended you purchase a hockey stick over the weekend. We will see you next Tuesday!'

Georgie walked past her classmates, standing tall and feeling proud of Elliot for defending himself and also her. In those few moments she knew it wouldn't be an easy ride at Northgate, but she'd be just fine. She wasn't a fan of lying to anyone but when it's for a good cause to bring bad people to justice she didn't see a great deal of harm in it. She just hoped Elliot got out unscathed at the end of the day, without getting challenged by Dillon and Carl.

As Georgie got outside, she breathed a sigh of relief that it was a Friday and luckily for her the school had an inset day planned giving her the Monday off also. Three days of stretching her legs in a new town with a new friend. She slumped into her dad's car and strapped on her seatbelt.

'How'd it go? I know it's bit of a drop from the old country college, but do you reckon it'll be okay?'

'It'll be fine Dad, Elliot is in my class. I'm sure we'll look out for each other.'

Thomas started the car and they drove out towards the school gates. Georgie looked back at the school and thought to herself; adventure one, survive Northgate.

Elliot had calmed down and his adrenaline levels seemed to be back to normal. Dillon and Carl both sat at their desk holding wet paper towels to their faces occasionally looking over at Elliot, this time however they weren't laughing. Elliot was a little disappointed in himself, he'd lost control and in front of someone who he really wanted to be friends with. He was worried he'd gone and ruined his chances before they had even got to know each other. Dispirited he looked down at his desk and grabbed the pen he lent to Georgie. He noticed she had written something on her piece of paper, but it wasn't Pythagoras' theorem. It simply read - 'Thank you, see you at 4!'

Elliot folded up the paper and slid it inside his jacket pocket.

CHAPTER FOUR
TROUBLE ON TWO STICKS

Northshore surgery was bursting at the seams with patients. Georgie managed to find an empty chair between an old man who looked as though he was falling asleep and a young mum who was helplessly trying to get her baby daughter to stop crying. Georgie found it hard to hear herself think over the loud coughs, sneezes and constant hum of chat that filled the waiting room. Every few minutes a patient would walk out with a prescription in hand and at the same time the receptionist would tilt open her glass divider and call out the next patients name, informing them that their doctor was ready to see them. Georgie only noticed two doctors' names on the plaque outside when she had arrived and it was apparent that her father's services were in desperate need. Much like Northgate Comprehensive, the surgery of a once very small town was expanding beyond its basic services. As she sat there, she started to feel a little anxious as memories of sitting in waiting rooms with her mum when they were diagnosing her illness came flooding back. She was so proud of her dad and how after a relatively short break he easily got back into the medical world after being surrounded by it twenty-four hours a day at home. His compassion and care for others was an inspiration to Georgie and how diligent he was at his job inspired her to work extra hard at school. Her dad was a very organised and neat person and liked everything to be in order. From alphabetising his record collection and keeping the house straight on his own. Right down to simple things like his immaculate handwriting, a rare occurrence for a doctor. He always told Georgie that if you're organised everything gets done quickly and efficiently, which leaves more time for fun things. Georgie always applied this ethic to her homework and got it out of the way immediately after school, allowing her the rest of the evening or weekend to herself.

Sitting in the waiting room reading the various posters about influenza and other illnesses on the notice board was making Georgie feel a little nauseated and she hoped her dad would appear soon. The only hint of colour or interest to her on the notice board was a 'don't take up smoking' ad campaign aimed at young people featuring Superman and the dastardly villain 'Nick O'Teen'. Georgie must have read the small comic strip on the poster fifty times and it reminded her of watching the Superman movie back home as a family and how much she enjoyed it. Her favourite character was Lois Lane, she liked how strong and independent a female character she was - even if she did need frequent rescuing from Superman. But she was a go-getter she always put herself out there to get the story and find out the truth for what she believed in. She also loved the music and how it made the hairs on the back of her neck stand up as the march took full throttle when Superman was in action. As much as she admired Lois Lane, Georgie quite fancied being Superman more. They had already been in there thirty minutes and she was now starting to feel a little claustrophobic and yearned to be outside breathing in the fresh air. Sitting in a stuffy waiting room full of sick people wasn't what she had anticipated and hoped for a bit of freedom to wander around the town, but her dad wanted to take her to lunch and promised he wouldn't take long. Glancing at her watch once more out of sheer boredom, Georgie looked up to see her dad walking towards her looking sheepish.

'Sorry sweetheart I didn't expect to get so swamped today, it was supposed to be a quick meeting. I'm going to have my hands full here for a few weeks before we calm things down by the look of it. I've suggested they hire a locum doctor to help out for a month too, looking at the patient numbers.' Her dad seemed excited to get stuck into a new project, Georgie could tell as his eyes seemed to light up when he spoke enthusiastically about something.

'It's okay, let's go eat lunch before I come down with a serious case of norovirus or contract the flu! Or worse still I could end up like him.' Georgie gestured at the old man who was now snoring next to her, her dad gently woke him up and checked he was OK. The old man laughed and offered his hand up to Thomas for a high five. Thomas lifted his hand and received a hearty high five and the three of them laughed, it was good timing as the man then finally got called in for his appointment.

As Georgie and Thomas left the surgery a man grabbed hold of Thomas' arm as they were walking past. Georgie flinched thinking the man was about to cause trouble, when she noticed he was smiling with his mouth wide open, showing pretty much all of his large jet white teeth.

'Rivers! What the heck are you doing back here, I thought you'd escaped?' the man said excitedly.

'Simo! Long-time no see!' Thomas replied, now laughing and shaking the man's hand as they both patted each other on their shoulders affectionately. Georgie relaxed and thought to herself that she'd never get any lunch at this rate. An hour later sitting around a small round table in a busy café opposite the surgery, Georgie munched her way through a large serving of gammon, egg and chips avoiding the pineapple that she had scraped off the top of the gammon. There was a strong smell of coffee and baked beans, it was a typical greasy spoon and her dad loved hanging out in them. He always told her it was a great place to people watch and that you'd never find a more down to earth place to dine at. Georgie would have preferred going to a burger joint like Wimpy or McDonald's, but Northshore didn't cater too well for the younger generations and was still firmly set in the sixties when it came to dining out. Her father and as it turned out old school friend Simon Jenkins who had joined them, were too busy talking and catching up on years past to eat their food at a normal rate. Simon had filled Thomas in on how he had been left his father's successful property business and was running it alongside his small tool hire company. Thomas was so used to telling people about his wife's illness and everything they'd had to deal with, that even Georgie knew his go to script and could fairly closely predict exactly what he'd say. Simon had the usual remorseful reaction to the news, but thankfully managed to somehow segue back into talking about himself, which Thomas was happy to hear.

Georgie had pieced together that Simon and her father hung around in the same group of friends, her dad was quite popular in school and had many social circles but didn't really have one best friend which he said he always regretted. From their conversation it turned out Simon had known her dad through the school football team, she hadn't realised her dad had been in a football team let alone the town's most successful goalkeeper. Simon had accurately and excitedly recalled every game they played together for two years, from when they turned sixteen, up until when her father left for university. At the end of their final season they were all awarded special signet rings from their coach and Simon still proudly wore his. It was made from cheap plated gold and featured the school insignia that Georgie had seen earlier that day mounted on the school gate. Simon took great pleasure in showing her the ring up close and teased Thomas for not wearing his anymore, although Georgie could completely understand why. It was quite garish and something only the likes of a teenager would have admired. Simon was clearly a man who liked to live in the past and Georgie wondered if he had ever strayed further than Northshore his entire life.

Simon had told Thomas about all the properties he now owned around the town and how much of a burden it was to him when they became empty. Only half of the properties it turned out were fully owned by his deceased father, the rest were still owned by the bank with hefty mortgages left to pay. Simon was considering selling off a few of the expensive ones, but he enjoyed having a monopoly over the town and didn't want to put his dad's reputation to shame by letting them go. He told Thomas of the car body shop unit he had sat there empty for nearly a year after an old friend of his had failed at making their car repair business a success. It had lost him a lot of money as a result until recently, a lady from out of town had paid six months' rent up front in cash to use it. Normally he'd only allow a minimum of a year contract on his commercial properties, but he had become desperate to keep the unit on his books and the offer of six months' rent was too good an opportunity to refuse. After initially seeming happy about the deal and welcoming the idea of a worry free six months, Simon's mood changed slightly, and he became a little distant, the glow that had been emanating from his face faded as he talked about the property and he looked a little burdened. He confessed that after a meeting at the unit earlier in the morning to hand over some spare keys, he was starting to wonder if he had done the right thing. He described the brand new 4x4 and the cold nature of the man who greeted him. A rather intimidating huge American, who seemed to want nothing but for Simon to go away as quickly as possible. He had noticed ropes, shovels and long military looking kit bags in the back of the Land Rover and couldn't help but think it was leading to bad news that he didn't want to be associated with. Georgie's dad tried to ease his concerns with potential sensible explanations and Simon agreed, he was probably just interrupting a busy meeting at the time and they were more than likely completely above board with whatever business they had in Northshore.

'If he was American maybe he hadn't long arrived and was still shaking off jet lag? Flying back from our honeymoon in San Francisco really hit me for a few days. By the sounds of the gear you described they're probably on an archaeological dig somewhere local. There's always plenty of Roman artefacts dotted around these parts aren't there?' Thomas asked.

'Yeah, you're probably right, they found some roman brooches last year close to the beach it was on the news, worth two million pounds apparently. Probably jumping on the back of that bandwagon, hey I may ask them if I can tag along!' Simon then admitted he liked to worry about nothing sometimes and his mood changed back to being relaxed and playful.

The idea of roman brooches and coins being found in the area grabbed Georgie's interest too and she thought maybe she could convince Elliot to go metal detecting down on the beach with her over the weekend, treasure hunting. Georgie was starting to get a little tired of grown up talk but managed not to let it show. It was nice for her to see her dad smiling and relaxed for a change and as brash and noisy Simon was, she liked him and could tell he was a kind man. She hoped that maybe her dad would get to spend some more time with Simon and rekindle some of his other old friendships in the town. Simon insisted on settling the lunch bill to Thomas' objections and as they left the café he invited Thomas and Georgie around to his house to meet his wife and two sons for dinner one evening. Thomas happily accepted, and Simon wrote his home telephone number down on the back of one of his business cards and handed it to him.

Georgie and Thomas headed back to the surgery where her dad's car was still parked, Georgie took in the sights and sounds of Northshore as they slowly walked back. She'd never seen so many seagulls as she had being here and didn't expect them to be congregating in the town centre, aggressively squawking at the passers-by sounding to Georgie like a ludicrous car alarm. The coast was a couple of miles out from the town, but the bins and a chance of an easy meal still attracted the birds. They slightly unnerved Georgie and she felt like she was being studied by them, their white piercing eyes focussed on her as she walked past two of them perched on a low wall. If Georgie had a phobia it was certainly bird related, something about larger birds horrified her and she didn't trust them to not attack her at any moment. She knew she was being ridiculous and always told herself that, but she could never shift the disgust or fear when she was in close proximity to them. As long as they stayed in the sky and further than arm's reach of her she was happy with that. As they approached the town's petrol station Thomas decided to pop in to grab a copy of the day's newspapers, he wasn't particularly fussed on tabloids but was always keen to follow what was happening in the world of sports. Georgie now knowing he was a keen footballer in his younger years could understand her dad's interest a lot more clearly, she thought it was just a typical 'Dad' thing to do.

Georgie decided to wait outside and stood at the front of the shop reading the headlines across the other newspapers sat in the paper rack, stacked next to the cheap flowers and empty petrol cans. The headlines were still dominated by the fall of the Berlin Wall in Germany. Headlines like 'It's Wall Over', 'Together at Last' and the one that stood out the most to her 'Freedom!'. Georgie being a typical twelve year old hadn't paid a huge amount of attention to world news. Obviously, she hadn't avoided it completely. She had seen snippets here and there during the news section of TV-am, the morning breakfast show that was always on in the background while they both busily got themselves ready in the mornings. But standing there now she started to wonder what it must have felt like. Divided from each other by a huge concrete wall covered in barbed wire, with soldiers positioned armed and ready guarding the checkpoints. She pictured them making sure nobody attempted to climb across illegally and if they did, they would get shot immediately.

The families and friends who got violently separated, divided by this huge concrete wall must have experienced so much despair and fear. Georgie got lost in her own world staring at the headlines trying to think what it would have been like if she had got separated from her parents and how that would have made her feel. A wave of emotion and sympathy came over Georgie and she found herself frozen to the spot. Georgie knew that World War Two had ended in 1945, yet here she was standing in front of newspapers nearly forty-five years later and its impact was still very present and still making headlines.

As Georgie stood there motionless trying to process her thoughts, a seagull had quietly glided down and landed behind her. The bird had noticed a discarded bread roll on the floor just to the side of Georgie's feet, it bobbed its head back and forth examining the bread for a moment deciding its best course of action before naturally letting out a giant screech of a caw, repeating like a high-pitched alarm. Georgie leapt forwards with fright and at that precise moment clashed into a man exiting the garage shop hitting him on the chin with her head. She managed to knock him straight off his feet and he fell backwards hard into the newspaper stand sending papers falling all around him. The man was on crutches which had fallen to his side and his foot was in a cast. Georgie felt embarrassed and couldn't quite believe what had just happened. She quickly jumped to her feet apologising and picked up the crutches to help the man. Her apologies fell on deaf ears as the man was furious. He grabbed at the scruff of her neck as she leant over him to help and used her to pull himself up, nearly pulling Georgie over in the process. He stank of coffee and cigarettes and he spat in Georgie's face as he gave her a tirade of verbal abuse. When he was fully back on his feet he grabbed one of the crutches to steady himself, while still firmly holding Georgie in his grasp. Georgie was surprised but not frightened, her adrenaline had kicked in and she kicked out at his injured leg and swiped his hand away from her neck. With this the man grabbed his second crutch out of Georgie's hand and raised it high in the air to strike her. Georgie raised her hands to protect herself when a huge man appeared and caught the crutch in one hand as it swung down towards her.

Georgie was shocked at the size of the man but was thankful he was there to help. Just as he was about to speak, Thomas came running out of the shop and stepped in front of Georgie protectively.

'What the hell is going on?!' he shouted, 'Georgie are you okay?'

Georgie nodded to say yes, but she couldn't manage to get any words out as she was still in shock from the attack. The huge man steadied the smaller angry man on his crutches and held him by his shoulder.

'Please excuse my friend here, I saw exactly what happened. He's a little sore over his broken ankle. He uh ... he got run over recently and since then he's a little easy to startle. He was however way out of line there and I think he owes you an apology. Don't you Dom?'

The huge man spoke with an American accent. He looked straight into the eyes of the injured man. Under his breath the smaller man spat 'Idiot petit fou aveugle.' The large American squeezed at the man's shoulder and he spoke up in English.

'Maybe you should be more aware of your surroundings in future. I apologise for grabbing you, as my friend says, I was a little over startled. Still in shock from my accident.'

He tapped at his cast as he spoke, and Thomas dusted down Georgie and checked her over, he looked in her eyes and asked if she was okay before turning back angrily to face the men.

'Apology accepted, I don't think the police will need to be informed this time. Maybe you should work on your anger a little though pal, she's twelve years old.' he said.

Thomas held Georgie's hand and stood with her slightly behind him.

'I agree Sir thank you for your understanding and again please accept our apologies, you have a nice weekend now.'

The hulking American turned himself and 'Dom' around and Georgie noticed they were walking toward a brand-new Land Rover parked next to one of the petrol pumps. The American helped the other man into the back of the car and then took his place at the driver's seat.

'You sure you're okay love, he seemed like a nasty piece of work. What happened exactly?' Georgie's father asked.

'One of those stupid birds frightened me and it made me jump right into him. I tried to help him up, but he went crazy. Sorry Dad.'

Thomas looked concerned and turned back to look at the Land Rover, it pulled forward and out of the petrol station driving past them. Georgie noticed in the front passenger seat an elegant looking woman who also had long red hair. She was shouting angrily to the man in the back seat. She stopped for a moment and turned to look at Georgie through the car window, making eye contact as they passed. She stared frostily into Georgie's eyes making her feel insignificant and foolish. As they pulled out onto the road Georgie pulled at her dad's hand.

'Dad, you know who those people are don't you?'

Thomas slightly shook his head in confusion looking puzzled.

'The Land Rover, the big American guy. That's who Simon was talking about. They're the ones who've rented his garage or whatever it is.'

It looked to Georgie as though a lightbulb had been turned on in her father's head and he was now on the same page as her.

'You're right, there can't be many around by that description. I'll let Simon know. Luckily no harm done, let's get you home.'

Georgie looked down at the crease in her t-shirt, Northshore in one day had exposed her to more trouble than she had experienced in most of her life. The incident at the school and now this, she was beginning to feel that maybe she had moved to the wrong town. Or that she wasn't quite cut out to live here and would be better suited back in her sleepy village in England. In the safety of her father's car she looked out of the window trying to take in the sights, especially the buildings to try and shake off the attack. She had never seen so many rows of terraced houses, all identical to each other apart from the painted coloured brickwork around the windows and the colour of the front doors. She really tried to control her emotions but couldn't help feeling a little empty inside and hadn't liked the realisation that she wasn't invulnerable after being pushed around by the man. She could still smell his breath as she pictured him forcefully holding onto her, hurling abuse at her in French and then seeing him raise his crutch to hit her. Georgie could understand some basic French but what he shouted at her was so fast and volatile she struggled to understand or hear what he was saying, which was probably a good thing.

When they arrived back at their new home, Thomas worryingly checked Georgie over once more. He was satisfied she hadn't come to any serious harm, but still checked her for bruises or scratches even though she protested. One thing he knew for certain was that his daughter was a tough cookie and could give as good as she got. He questioned himself and wondered if he should have called the police to report the man. But he knew what the local police at Northshore were like and if nobody got hurt or no property was damaged, then they would have only convinced both parties to apologise and move on. Very little happened in Northshore that managed to attract police attention, the less they needed to get involved the better it was for them.

Georgie went up to her room to get changed into her 'muck about' clothes as her mum used to call them, ready for her meet up with Elliot. Torn old jeans, old leather Puma trainers and a long sleeve blue and yellow jersey with the words Raleigh Burner emblazoned in bright yellow on the chest. The shirt had come with her bike as a freebie and she thought Elliot would like it. It was a little too big but once she put on her elbow pads she thought it looked half decent. Her dad knocked on the door and wandered in, armed with a tape measure.

'Hey, BMX bandit!' He said jokingly, mocking Georgie's attire. 'Give us a hand with these windows before you head out, will you? I'll pop out to the store and get some cheap rails and curtains in the morning.' he said.

'You okay with me going out for a bit after what happened earlier Dad? I don't mind if you want me to stay in?' Georgie replied earnestly.

'Sweetheart I'm sure you'll be fine, Elliot seems like a nice kid and that dog of his will look after the pair of you I'm sure! If you come across that man again try not to barge into him or kick his dodgy leg!'

Georgie laughed awkwardly rolling her eyes and walked over to help measure up her window. Her doubts from earlier had eased and she began to feel excited about getting out and exploring the town her way. Having her dad around was always fine but she needed to let her hair down and get her bearings ready for when she started school the following week. Elliot had told her that the other kids tended to get lunch off school premises at lunch times, they'd buy chips from the nearby fish and chip shop or café and she wanted to know first-hand where these places were. It was twenty past three, Elliot would be finishing school soon. She couldn't help but wonder if he would manage to escape unscathed from Northgate, after his earlier antics with the bullies and the book.

CHAPTER FIVE
DISCOVERIES IN THE DARK

Elliot nervously awaited the school bell. He had sat through the last two hours of double chemistry, comfortable in the knowledge that Carl Coombes and Dillon Davies were on the other side of the building in the biology block. He never understood why the science classrooms were separated in Northgate. His previous school in Cardiff had them all sectioned together down a long dark corridor in the same part of the school. Two classrooms were allocated for physics, two for chemistry and one for biology. All of them had unique smells depending on what chemicals or wildlife were currently residing in them. It proved useful for Elliot having all the science classes clustered together. So long as he knew he had science, it was hard for him to be in the wrong place. There were numerous rumours for the separation of the classrooms between the pupils at Northgate, some that were quite ridiculous. The favourite being that the chemistry and biology teachers were once married but suffered a horrible divorce due to the stresses of working at the school and dealing with its difficult pupils. It was said that the Headmistress was given an ultimatum from them that she either separated the science blocks, so they didn't have to see each other, or lose their talents to rival schools. Something Ms James couldn't afford to do. So, she accepted the request and rejigged the school classrooms just for them. Elliot however knew this not to be the case, he had seen Mr Hicks and Mrs Stone chatting quite happily plenty of times. He knew the rumour was just that, a story made up by one of the students no doubt and one all the teachers were completely oblivious to. One story Elliot did believe was that the students used to leave the gas taps on in the chemistry lab intentionally to upset the teachers. A few years ago, it had led to a small explosion that killed the fish and other small animals they kept there, like guinea pigs and hamsters in the adjacent biology class. Ms James being a strict vegan and animal rights activist was distraught and initiated the move herself as to never let any more animals get harmed there again. She also banned the dissecting of frogs and the use of Bunsen burners and ordered that all the gas taps were blocked up. Something most of the children complained about regularly knowing their older brothers and sisters had the chance to enjoy the more practical lessons years prior. It seemed now that Elliot mainly copied out of textbooks and studied diagrams hastily drawn on the blackboard by burned out disillusioned teachers.

The clock seemed to be taking forever to reach three thirty. Elliot knew that with the two bullies being on the other side of school the quicker he made it out of his side of the building the better chance he had of avoiding them. He sat there watching the large clock at the front of the class, the second hand slowly but surely moving the minute hand from twenty-seven past to twenty-eight past. Just two minutes left. Elliot's legs nervously swayed back and forth while he quietly packed his books and pencil case into his rucksack. He hoped Mr Hicks didn't notice, but he seemed to be winding the class down, ready for his weekend to start also. Elliot was confident he would get away with it. One more minute to go. Elliot now looked around the full classroom to see if his escape route was clear. There were bags on the floor next to the students' feet and he noticed a few others had started to sneakily pack away too. But his path looked clear. He would be out of the classroom in two seconds, down the hallway narrowly avoiding the other pupils spilling out of physics, then straight past the geography rooms. Then just after the toilets he'd escape through the school's heavy double doors… to freedom. He stared at the clock one more time while tapping his finger nails on the desk. Then like a gun at the start of a race, the bell screamed throughout the school. Elliot sprinted up out of his seat and ran as fast as he could down the corridor. His path was clear, he got through in a flash. As he turned the corner to pass the geography classes he hadn't anticipated the eagerness of the other students to get out as quickly as they had, then he remembered how boring the geography classes were. He hit the student bodies like a slow-moving wall and felt like he was crawling slowly through treacle. He could see the toilets, the double doors, freedom merely feet away.

His time came, and he finally reached the outside, the cool air enveloping his face. He gave a quick scan left and right to make sure Carl or Dillon weren't already flanking him. The coast looked clear and he ran full speed for the small less popular entrance at the side of the school. None of the busses were parked at this gate and it was always the more sensible exit if you were walking, or in this case running home. He chose his path wisely and he managed to escape unscathed. Thankfully the school lollipop lady dressed to the hilt in 'high-vis' gear, already had the traffic under her control and he made it across the road and into the lanes and back alleys of Northshore in record time. He confidently slowed his run to a jog, then a brisk walk knowing his tormentors were now queuing to get on their bus to take them on their four-mile journey home to the next village of Sambrook Bay.

Elliot relaxed knowing he was safe for the weekend, he looked down at his feet and kicked an empty coke can up the lane scoring an imaginary goal. He could unwind now after a day of tension at the school and he couldn't wait to see Georgie. As he wandered alone through the town he liked to pretend he was a secret agent by avoiding as many of the main roads as he could. Choosing instead to stick to the back lanes where most of the terraced houses accessed their garages and back gardens - thus avoiding being captured by the villain in his imaginative storyline. The lanes were always quiet, the entire time he'd been at Northshore he'd rarely come across another person walking through them at home time. So, he would hide in garage doorways, then dart out across the lane to hide behind lamp posts and fences, holding his fingers together in the shape of a gun. Elliot had discovered that when you're lonely, your imagination can be a true friend. In no time he would be at the street leading to his estate and his little game would be over, as he walked out onto the main road and back into public view. Passing a small community centre and a block of flats purpose built for the elderly or 'granny flats' as everyone called them, the entrance to his estate looked a lot more welcoming today than it usually did. Georgie was already out on the street performing endos and bunny hops on her BMX. Elliot couldn't believe what he was seeing, this girl could really ride! He watched as she built up some speed, bunny hopped over the curb onto the roundabout, then went straight into a stoppie finishing off with a 180 turn only to come to a halt while still in control of her bike. Standing there balancing on the pedals she looked up, waved with a free hand and cycled towards Elliot pulling a perfect wheelie in the process.

'Nice moves!' he said enthusiastically.

'Thanks! I think my tyres need a bit of air though, I can't find which box the pump is in. Can I borrow yours?'

'Sure! I'll just quickly get changed and be right out, gimme a sec!' Elliot replied while running to his house. He could already hear Chinook's excited loud bark as he got to his driveway.

Elliot sped in through the front door immediately letting the excited dog out into the back garden to stretch his legs. He quickly put his food bowl down from the worksurface which he'd prepared early that morning, knowing it would save him valuable time after school. Littering his uniform across the house as he went, his play clothes were already waiting for him along with his old trainers on the living room sofa. He knew he'd get an earful off his mum when she arrived home with Alice and she'd end up having to tidy away his uniform. But he wanted to get as much time in with Georgie before needing to be home for dinner at five pm. Friday night was always pizza and chips night in the Cassley household, an institution still ingrained from when his dad was a part of the family. Elliot was dressed and ready to go in record time and hurriedly grabbed the garage keys while locking the back door behind him. Georgie was waiting at the gate at the end of his driveway and Chinook wasted no time in greeting her by lifting his giant front paws up onto the gate and licking the air in front of her face affectionately. Georgie removed her BMX glove and scratched at Chinooks throat making his tail wag furiously and causing his back leg to rise off the ground, beginning to 'air scratch' as a result. This made Georgie laugh out loud, Elliot whistled at Chinook and he jumped down allowing Georgie to open the gate and wheel her bike toward the garage at the opposite end of the driveway.

Georgie rested her bike up against the wall while Elliot opened the up and over red garage door. Georgie turned and peered into a very busy garage with boxes stacked against the walls, push bikes of various sizes and the usual decades old lawn mower and tools messily stored in the corner. What Georgie wasn't expecting to see in the middle of it all, was a pristine looking Kawasaki KX 80cc motocross bike on its stand. Georgie's eyes widened at the sight of it, she thought it was glorious. With a bright green fuel tank featuring KX 80 graphics emblazoned down the side and a dark blue seat, this was the embodiment of an adventurous twelve-year olds dream possession. For years Georgie had fantasized about trying an off-road motocross bike but had only ever seen them in magazines, a dodgy American TV movie called 'The Dirt Bike Kid' and on the closer to home television show 'kickstart'. Watching the show, she was always in awe at the skill of the riders managing to overcome various log and barrel obstacles on their trials bikes and only last year she'd watched the British round of the 1988 500cc world championship motocross highlights on a sports show with her dad. The sound of the powerful bikes as they screamed around a sand course, tearing up the ground and spewing out the dirt behind the back wheel. It was a fast-paced dangerous sport and Georgie loved the look of it.

'Whose bike is that?!' she exclaimed.

'Oh, that. That's my guilt gift.' Elliot replied morosely.

'What do you mean? It's fantastic!' Georgie couldn't hold back her excitement, charging into the garage and inspecting the bike up close running her hand down the tank and over the seat.

'I used to ride with my dad. When he left us, he bought me that out of guilt, so we call it my guilt gift.' Elliot pulled down his bicycle pump from a shelf and handed it to Georgie.

'It goes like stink to be fair. Frightens me actually, it's too powerful. I still have my old 50cc Suzuki at the back there.' he pointed to the back wall of the garage where a smaller older yellow motorbike had become a shelf for his mums many washing baskets.

'He took me out on it once before we moved away but kept getting annoyed with me stopping as I couldn't handle it very well. So, he cut our session short and brought me home. I haven't used it or seen him since. My mum wants me to sell it, but I dunno. I want to be able to ride it one day, to prove him wrong I guess. I'll stick to the BMX for now though!'

Georgie completely understood, and she felt a little bad for getting so excited by it, not knowing Elliot's reaction would be so gloomy. She tried to put a positive spin on the conversation.

'Hey maybe you could let me borrow the old Suzuki one day and you can use the KX to teach me?'

'Maybe, we'd need to get you a proper helmet first, I've only got the one. Let's get your tyres sorted and hit the road I've got a great place I want to show you.'

Elliot helped Georgie get her tyres inflated by holding the bike upright for her. He was impressed by how well she knew the components of her bike and didn't expect her to be so quick and hands on with it. Most of his other friends always left that up to their parents to fix. She finished pumping up the tyres and used the base of her hand to check if they were firm enough. Elliot tossed the pump back into the garage and slammed the door shut. Chinook barked excitedly as they both jumped onto their saddles and pushed off out of Elliot's drive onto the road. Elliot couldn't resist showing off some of his moves, using the drop curbs as little jumps and standing on his stunt pegs at the back of his bike, freewheeling down the hill heading into town. Georgie enjoyed having someone who seemed to have so much in common with her living across the road. Of all the bad experiences she'd already had at Northshore, Elliot outweighed them all.

Elliot signalled for Georgie to follow him as he banked left down a lane leading to what she could see were industrial buildings. The road turned from smooth tarmac to gravel and stone, making the terrain more difficult to control her bike on. Slowing her bike down weary of the surface, Georgie hoped Elliot would turn around and notice her hesitance as he had ridden quite far ahead. Luckily, he turned and noticed that the distance had grown between them and he hit his back-brake skidding and turning 180 degrees to face her, impressively kicking up a cloud of dust and throwing small bits of gravel to the side.

'Sorry, I slowed down in case there's any trucks or lorries about.' Georgie said through her helmet her voice slightly muffled by her mouth guard.

'It's okay I think all the units shut at four, I've never come across any trucks. We can take our time though we're nearly there.' he said happily.

Chinook was off exploring and sniffing around the bushes and lamp posts, but always popped his head up now and again to check his owner and new friend were close by.

Georgie was a little surprised when Elliot hopped off his bike and started to walk with it into a heavily built up area of brambles, stingy nettles and tree cover to the side of a fence that had a huge steel gate locked at the front. After the trouble she had already experienced today, she was reluctant to encounter any more. Elliot turned and signalled with his head for her to follow and with Chinook at her side, she pushed her bike into the unwelcoming foliage, thinking if she didn't fancy it she could always turn back. Walking between the fence and a slight drop to a small stream below, she wondered where Elliot was taking her. She didn't have to wait very long to find out. Elliot had stopped and pulled apart a hole that had been cut in the chain link fence before pushing his bike through with his free hand. Being close to the trees and the drop to the stream below the owners hadn't worried about repairing it, thinking the drop must have been a deterrent enough. Elliot had discovered it on one of his long walks with Chinook and braved bringing his bike down a few weeks later. Once he was through he pulled the opening wider to allow Georgie to get through without snagging her clothes or handle bars and Chinook quickly followed behind into Elliot's very own private BMX course. It was a playground of sand, gravel and mounds of earth, all heavily compacted so you could ride a BMX over them and not worry about it collapsing under the wheels. There were barrels and wood beams, even a JCB with its bucket resting on the floor at the front of the giant yellow machine, just perfect for climbing on and jumping off with the bikes. Elliot had carried over some of the wooden beams and propped them up on the large iron bucket creating obstacles and ramps for him and Georgie to ride down and jump over.

They had a great time together and even though they had gotten a little overzealous with their risk taking and crashed a few times, they just dusted themselves off and got straight back into it. Fortunately, only suffering minor grazes and bruises. Georgie managed to pull off a 360-turn landing her bike briefly before skidding out and collapsing hard to the gravel floor face first, with her legs twisted around the frame of her bike it looked like a nasty fall. Elliot rushed over to see if she was okay only to find her ecstatic and laughing that she finally managed to do it after many attempts, although she confessed she may not try it again for a little while as she pulled herself up. Elliot was holding Georgie's bike and she noticed her front wheel had been knocked out of line with the frame. Without hesitating, she put the front wheel in between her knees and turned the handlebars back to their original position.

'I'll have to get my dad to help tighten that up tomorrow, should be okay to get home though.' she said before inspecting her handlebar stem.

'Yeah, it'll be fine, you sure you're alright?' Elliot replied still concerned.

Georgie noticed the inside of her thigh was tender from the fall, but she kept it to herself. The frame of the bike must have done a little more damage than she first noticed, but the adrenaline was keeping most of the pain at bay and she was still buzzing from all the fun they had. The bruises she thought were definitely worth it and it was nothing a good bath probably couldn't help fix. After half an hour of solid BMX freestyle the light was quickly starting to fail, and they knew their time was up for the evening.

'We should probably head back, you okay to ride or shall we walk?'

'I'm fine El honestly, I've had worse than that before.' Georgie made it clear that Elliot didn't need to pamper her, and he got the message.

'Come on then, one last quick lap of the mounds and we'll get back!' he said.

They both pushed off tearing around the yard going over the earth and gravel mounds as quick as they could, while Chinook chased excitedly behind. Elliot aimed his bike for the fence and used his front wheel to slice through the opening, skidding to a halt and kicking up the dust from his back tyre.

As they exited at the side of the fence using their bikes to weigh down the brambles and stingy nettles on the ground, Georgie looked up and noticed Simon Jenkins' van parked outside the back of one of the industrial units opposite. As they cycled past heading home, Georgie glanced over to see if she could see Simon to shout 'hello', but the van was empty, and nobody seemed to be around. Elliot was buzzing from how much Georgie had enjoyed riding around his secret BMX course and couldn't wait to go there with her again. But there was a lot more to Northshore that he had to share with her over the coming days, including the beach that would take top priority. Georgie was curious if Simon had heard from her dad about the trouble with his new tenants earlier in the day and she was concerned the unit his van was parked at was the one they were renting from him. She really didn't want to be the cause of any trouble for Simon and hoped he hadn't decided to get involved. She tried to put it out of her mind and would ask her father on returning home if he had spoken to his old friend. Hopefully she thought, it was just a coincidence and Simon was probably just checking on one of his many properties in town before heading home to his family.

Simon had rung the bell and knocked the door of the old body shop for at least five minutes. He had peered through the window numerous times before he decided to use one of his back up keys that he kept on a large keychain in the glove box of his van. He had heard an hour ago that the people who had been seen using the unit had caused a fracas at the local petrol station with a young girl earlier in the day. He only had the Chinese whispers of the garage employees to go off. But the description matched that of the American he had met in the morning. He wanted to speak to his new tenants and get their side of the story. His business and reputation was very important to him and he didn't want these outsiders tainting it. He wouldn't stand for being responsible for bringing trouble makers into the town and he wanted to make that crystal clear from the start. He also had his own doubts about the people he was now doing business with and it was playing heavily on his mind. He was certain nobody was in the unit and decided to investigate what they were doing for himself.

Using his set of spare keys, he slowly entered the dark unit. He chose not to turn on the lights but use a flashlight that he always kept in his van for emergencies. Looking around the ground floor of the unit everything looked as it should, even the old motoring adverts for tyres and exhausts were still hung on the walls. It made sense, they hadn't been using the building more than a few days. Simon shone the torch around the huge empty room but stopped when the light hit the locks on the roller shutter doors. He noticed something was different. Simon walked over and inspected two brand new padlocks that had replaced the rusty old ones that he knew had been there for years, yet still worked perfectly. The replacement locks looked very expensive and were master combination operated, meaning you'd need a complex code to unlock them. This was pretty serious security he thought, he wondered if anything else had been changed. He shone the torch around the surround of the roller shutter door not being aware of the silent alarm he had triggered minutes prior when he opened the smaller main entrance door. Simon's suspicions grew seeing the replacement locks, it seemed very overkill for the quiet town of Northshore. What were they planning on keeping in the unit? As he aimed the flashlight on the stairs leading up to the office, he couldn't resist but to investigate further. Doubtful in his assumptions, he hesitated thinking to himself of the old saying 'curiosity killed the cat' and that he should probably just head home and come back tomorrow when they were in. Simon's distrust got the better of him, something didn't add up with these people and he had to find out what, even if it meant snooping through their things a bit further. He glanced out of the window at his van and then out of the front window as well, the coast was still clear. He called out, 'Hello, anybody around? Landlord visit!' His voice reverberated around the building and no reply came back. What was upstairs he thought?

Slowly keeping the beam of the torch on the stairs he climbed up to the office. His steel toe capped boots were difficult to keep silent on the metal staircase, loudly clanging one step at a time. As he entered the office he noticed four black kit bags with what seemed to be heavy equipment inside them. The bag's zips were again secured with smaller combination locks, so he couldn't open them to see what they were hiding inside. He tried lifting one of them to check the weight and was surprised by how heavy it was, barely raising it an inch off the floor. Whoever carried these up the stairs was either very strong or it was a two-man job. Turning his attention to the desk, he noticed a stack of black and white photographs of what appeared to be a cave. They were very dark photos with some featuring a man he didn't recognise standing in front of what looked like an old doorway recessed into the cave wall. Rifling through the photos he noticed someone had written on them with a chinagraph pencil, the words glowing white as he shone his flashlight at the reflective paper. The words had arrows pointing to certain parts of the photographs, with circles highlighting certain areas. Simon read the handwritten notes that said, 'no dynamite to be used', 'door must open from behind?', 'may need a child to climb through'.

A child? Simon got a cold chill down the back of his spine and dropped the photographs on the floor, disturbing the months' worth of dust that had built up there. He stood there staring at the photos as they fell. What were these people planning? Where were these photos taken? Who was that man in the picture? Simon could feel his heart starting to pound, it felt like his entire body was throbbing. His throat started to tighten, and panic was starting creep through. Simon edged himself backwards from the desk, he needed to call the police and he needed to call them immediately. He knew all along there was something sinister about these people. He raised his flashlight pointing it at the desk, his eyes quickly scanned for a telephone. There wasn't one. Aiming his torch along the skirting board at the bottom of the wall he saw an empty telephone socket. Simon knew there was a pay phone just up the street outside the post office, he'd run as fast as he could and call from there. As Simon turned to run, his torch slipped out of his hand onto the floor and it rolled away from him. He tripped over, landing on his knees and hands and quickly scrambled to grab it. As he handled the torch his thumb hit the power switch and it turned off. It was as though he had been plunged into a black hole and he screamed internally. He stood up frantically thumbing at the torch to turn the light back on. Forgetting that the switch was faulty, he became even more flustered. Finally igniting the torch, the room lit up and he had to promptly calm himself down. Sweat was pouring out of him and he could feel his shirt sticking to his back. He knew he was overreacting, he told himself he was alone, and he knew he had to get himself together. He couldn't afford to trip down the metal stairs in his haste and injure himself. Simon stood still, closed his eyes and took in a deep breath and exhaled slowly repeating the words 'Calm down Simon, calm down.'

Thirty seconds must have passed while Simon got himself together and felt his heart rate start to slow down. He opened his eyes and noticed his hands were shaking. Time to move. He slowly made his way to the bottom of the staircase, he was a step closer to the front door when he heard a quick movement to his left. He spun the torch around in the direction of the scraping noise. It sounded like a foot dragging along the ground. There was nothing there. The torch started to flicker before it turned off completely. Dropping it in the office must have caused some damage or loosened the batteries and it was now malfunctioning. Simon found himself standing in the darkness, once again terrified.

'Oh, what now!' he said aloud and cursed under his breath.

Shaking the flashlight and repeatedly hitting it with his hand, he begged for the torch to ignite back to life. It flickered a few times before igniting fully just as Simon had a split second to see the face of the man from the photographs stood directly in front of him. Simon didn't have a chance to move or speak before the man brought down his right hand and smashed a crutch into the centre of Simons skull. Once again Simon was plunged into darkness, but this time with searing pain and this time, the darkness was permanent.

CHAPTER SIX
THE DRAGON'S EYE

Klaus Wolfgang peered through his spyglass and scanned the edge of the French coast. He saw two Royal Navy warships performing their daily drills a couple of miles out from the shoreline. This was a huge setback; his men were all eagerly awaiting their next instructions but knew they had to avoid the Royal fleet at all costs. It had been a long four weeks of sailing from the most southern point of Africa, stopping only for supplies in the dead of night. The crew were growing tired of life sailing the Dragon's Eye. Ever since the crew had taken aboard treasures and two crewmen from rival pirate ship The Good Grief, some of the men had been struck down with a strange illness and bizarre things were happening to the ship. The ratlines had snapped at night and the water reserves had been mysteriously contaminated with sea water. Klaus lowered his spyglass, then in a moment of rage and frustration threw it against the forecastle deck smashing the glass across the timber boards. He had hoped he could navigate his ship through the English Channel to arrive at his destination quickly to rid himself of the burden of his ship and his failing crew. He didn't dare challenge the might of the British fleet and it pained him knowing it would be safer to take a longer alternative route. He had already lost three of his men to this strange illness and he couldn't afford to lose anymore, the ship would be too difficult to sail with a dwindling crew. He knew he was close, Germany was only days away and he could reap the rewards of the treasure they had stolen, selling it on the black market that he knew so well back in his homeland. Something had felt wrong on the ship ever since taking the hoard from The Good Grief. Klaus was overcome by what felt like a great burden, he felt anxious and paranoid that his crew were planning on betraying him and starting a mutiny to take the riches for themselves. He tried to not let the pressure show and to look as though he was still in full command of the ship.

He knew it would be dangerous but with the advice of his first mate, Klaus chose to avoid the English Channel and instead travel up between Ireland and Wales through the Celtic and Irish seas. Sailing so close to the mainland was a risk and Klaus decided to wait for nightfall before setting sail. As the sun slowly went down a storm started to creep up on the ship. The waves became choppy and the ship swayed back and forth. Klaus paced around steadying himself on anything at arm's length as the waters became more turbulent. As he made his way across the deck he past his ill crewmen coughing blood into rags, trying to not let their illness defeat them. Painfully through the high winds they managed the ship readying it to set sail as soon as dusk had taken hold. Klaus knew that they would soon get worse. That they would start to convulse and haemorrhage from their nose and ears like the three poor souls that they had already thrown overboard days before. This would bring the death toll to seven. He decided it was time to interrogate the two crewmen from The Good Grief, hoping to shine some light on the origin of the stolen gold and diamonds sitting in the belly of the ship and if they had any clue of this deadly illness. From the infirmary at the stern to the stores at the bow he searched the ship high and low, yet there was no sign of the two crewmen. He probed his crew as to the men's location, but no one could remember seeing them for the last few hours.

Dangerous as it was in the high winds he climbed the main mast to the crow's nest at the top, the only place left to check. His hands slipped on the ropes and he fought desperately to keep his grip as the rain now started to lash down ferociously. As Klaus reached the crow's nest, he heaved his body over the brim falling into the bowl with a hard thud. He cried out in agony as he cracked his shoulder hard against the timber base. As he looked up wiping the rain clear of his eyes he scrambled to his feet drawing his cutlass from its scabbard, staring back at him were the two men from The Grief. Huddled together and soaking wet, the two men were terrified of the storm but it was clear they'd rather risk their lives up here than down below on deck.

'What's happening to my men, you know something! Answer me!' Klaus yelled over the distant thunder at the men, aiming his cutlass close to their faces. At first, they wouldn't answer, refusing to look Klaus in the eye.

Klaus grabbed the larger of the two crewmen by the throat and pressed his cutlass into the man's side. As he screamed out in pain the younger male on the floor who to Klaus' eye was merely a boy, called out.

'It's the box Captain! The gold box!'

Klaus released the larger, older man and he rolled over wincing, nursing his side. Klaus had barely given him a flesh wound, but he had turned the men's fear against them and used it to his advantage. Standing tall over the smaller pirate who was barely fourteen years old by Klaus' estimate, staring directly into his eyes he demanded more answers. The frightened young boy spoke up.

'The gold box Sir, the men who touched it on The Grief went the same way as your boys. It's cursed I tell 'ya! We don't even know what's in it but whatever it is ... we ... we don't want nuffin' to do with it!'

'How many men did The Grief lose before you figured this out?!'

'We lost eight Sir, eight before one of the men was clever enough to work it out. We were trying to figure out how to get rid of it, then you lot showed up shooting your cannons.'

Klaus looked at the fear in the men's faces and knew they were telling him the truth.

'You can't stay up here, come down with me now and stay in my quarters while I look at this box.'

Getting down the main mast was just as dangerous as getting up it, the storm was now very close, and the waves crashed onto the deck. Klaus found his first mate and ordered them to sail towards the Irish sea. The Dragon's Eye was plunged into the heavy waves as it used the strong winds to drive it's sail hard through the Celtic Sea. The men were sailing blind using only their compasses to help guide them away from the storm. Klaus headed for the officer's quarters and found two of his crew who were suffering the effects of the mystery illness.

'You two, come with me.' he ordered.

Staring at their Captain confused and dizzy from their illness, Klaus locked his eyes on the men until they both unwillingly got up, clutching their bloodied rags close to their mouths and followed him. With the ship swaying and getting consumed by the high waves, the men had to slowly battle their way across the deck before lowering themselves through the main hatch to the hold below. Klaus slammed the hatch shut behind him and ignited an extra oil lamp to light up the hold. The hoard of stolen treasures was stored in five large chests. Klaus ordered his two crewmen to open them all, as they did he walked behind them shining the lamp into each chest. He couldn't see a gold box easily, the chests seemed to be full of loose doubloons, large diamonds and rubies, but he wasn't willing to risk touching them with his own hands. He wondered if the crewmen from The Grief were playing a trick on him? He stood there doubting their story for a few seconds when the ship suddenly jolted to one side causing the chests to slide into each other, spilling some of their contents out onto the floor. Klaus and his men were knocked off their feet and his lamp fell out of his hands, landing dangerously close to falling down the inner hatch to where the ship's gunpowder stocks were stored. He reached out just catching it by the handle before it fell. Klaus' heart was pounding fast. He knew he had been lucky that time and that he needed to be more careful.

He shone the lamp back onto the chests and noticed that the jolt had revealed the corner of a gold box, hidden under the treasures of one of the chests. Klaus pointed to the chest and demanded the men pull the gold box out for him to see. Unaware of what their Captain knew and already ill from inadvertently handling the box via the chest, they both sank their hands into the riches and removed a heavy gold box and placed it in front of Klaus. The box made of solid gold was about half a meter long and seemed to quietly hum with a static noise. The three men looked at each other apprehensively. Taking a step back away from the box while keeping his eyes firmly on it, Klaus spoke out.

'Open it.' he ordered.

One of the men began coughing heavily and started to convulse on the floor. Seeing this the second crewmember started to panic and looked as though he was about to run for the hatch. Klaus blocked the stairs with his cutlass primed in his hand and again ordered that the box be opened. Reluctantly, the crew member dropped onto his knees and started to unclasp the box. As he opened it Klaus could see his sombre expression turn into elation before his eyes suddenly rolled back into his head and he collapsed next to the box causing the lid to shut. Klaus didn't know what to do. He stood there staring at it, knowing that if he touched it he'd possibly share the same fate as the men who had handled it before. Stepping over his two crewmen lying unconscious on the hold floor he quickly scooped up the spilt treasure tossing it back into the chests avoiding the gold box. Klaus stared at this beguiling box, it was a beautiful thing to behold but he daren't approach it. He stood rigid, trying to stay on his feet with the ship violently rocking back and forth as he considered his options. Should he get another unsuspecting, already condemned ill crewman to handle the box and throw it overboard? Or should he risk an attempt to see what's inside? He didn't get the chance to do either.

Above him the hatch door burst open and the hold was filled with the sound of the worsening storm above. His first mate Rodrigo came tumbling down the stairs.

'Captain! The main mast and the bowsprit have been struck by lightning sir. The ship is on fire.'

Klaus sprinted past Rodrigo and headed up to the poop deck. Considering the rain was so heavy, fire was taking hold at an alarming rate. Klaus couldn't understand how a sodden ship was managing to burn so quickly and ferociously in the middle of a storm. With every gust of high wind, the fire spread lower like an enraged Bengal tiger clawing its way down the mast to its prey. Klaus knew they had to abandon the ship and they had to move fast. The storm had knocked the Dragon's Eye off course and through the rain Klaus could see land in the distance. He ordered his men to retrieve the chests from the hold and to load it into the lifeboats. The storm may take the ship, but he refused to go down empty handed. Klaus joined his men in the hold and watched as one of his unsuspecting crew scooped up the gold box and placed it back into one of the chests. Klaus thought fast, drew out his dagger and threw it at the chest that now held box, as it pierced the wood his men turned around shocked.

'That chest… that chest goes in the last boat. Load the others first.' the closest crewman to the chest removed his dagger and offered it back to the captain.

'You can keep that. Let's get going.' he ordered.

The men barely made it off the ship with their lives and their struggle continued as they rowed the lifeboats to the shore, not knowing which shore or country they were sailing to. Klaus looked on as his ship was swallowed up by the ocean and his hopes of getting back to Germany anytime soon sunk as fast as the ship. Only four of the lifeboats made it to dry land with the remaining men waiting out the storm under cliffs on the unknown beach throughout the night. As dawn approached Klaus counted only four boats and four chests, one of the surviving chests bore the mark of his dagger.

His crew explored the beach and the surrounding cliffs and discovered a set of caves hidden behind a waterfall. Klaus now had only eight men at his disposal, including the two crew members taken from The Grief. Carefully he monitored who had come into contact with the chests. Noticing that The Grief's men had managed to avoid touching any of them opting to assist with other duties such as breaking down the lifeboats for wood to burn. As Klaus' crew didn't quite trust them they were happy to handle the treasures alone and were unaware of the mysterious gold box. Klaus ordered the men to move the four chests to the caves, it hadn't taken long before he had counted all six of his remaining crew had handled the marked chest. He knew it would be only twenty-four hours before they too started to succumb to the mystery illness.

Klaus inspected the caves and decided it would be safer to stash the treasure there before trying to move it across country, especially as they weren't entirely sure which country they were now marooned on. He had his men carry the chests and wood from the lifeboats deep into the caves. Luckily apart from the waterfall at the entrance, the caves were dry, and no seawater had penetrated through the cave wall. They would be safe here for years to come he thought, his men grew restless quickly and demanded a plan. Klaus offered only one option, he was to leave the men behind with the chests on guard while he and the men from The Grief walked to the nearest town to find supplies and hopefully, information. He knew his men wouldn't last longer than four days with their impending illness and no food. Klaus was greedy and wanted the men out of the picture to make sure he had a higher percentage of the stolen riches. Standing in the dark cave surrounded by his men and the chests, he ordered one of the men closest to the marked chest to open it and place a handful of coins into a small cloth bag that he tossed toward him. Burying his hand into the chest the man's fingers touched the box. Curious he pulled it out.

'What's this Captain?' he said.

Klaus pretended to look surprised as if he had no idea what the gold box was.

'I have no idea, please open it and let's see inside.'

Not needing to be asked twice the pirate unclasped the box and flipped the lid open. Laying inside the gold box resting on a bed of gold silk was a falcon shaped gold and pearl amulet. It was beautiful to behold and dazzled in the fire light. Klaus looked closer over the shoulder of the crewman and noticed hieroglyphics adorned the outside edge of the wings, the detail and construction was perfect. Klaus was mesmerised by the amulet but also terrified of its mysterious power and feared touching it. Not for the first time, Klaus hid his feelings away from his men.

'We're going to be filthy rich lads, no doubt about it. Put that back in the chest and keep your wits about you. We'll be back as soon as we can.'

Klaus drew the chords on the bag of loose coins and tossed them to the young boy from The Grief. He looked shocked to be given the responsibility of the money and Klaus winked at him putting his mind at ease. The two men and young ship hand headed out into the unknown darkness leaving the crew of the Dragon's Eye on guard at the cave. When they had been walking for some time the older crewman spoke up.

'You know they're not going to be breathing by the time we get back Captain? I was watching them, same as you, they all touched that chest.' he said morosely.

'Oh, I'm counting on it. We'll take our time now and when we return to the caves with the wood you reclaimed from the lifeboats we're going to construct a door. We'll barricade the treasure in until we can get a ship back to retrieve it all, including that amulet.'

The young boy looked shocked.

'But Captain, it has to be cursed we can't touch it!' he said trembling.

'Don't worry lad, we won't be touching it. We'll bring a new crew back with us to do all the lifting. We'll just be sure to bring plenty of them and make sure only two of them carry it onto the ship and another two carry it off. I know a man in my country who'd be very curious to see that amulet. He has a knowledge of black magic and curses, he may be able to help us. I just need to get it to him.'

Five days after setting out, Klaus and the two men returned to the caves. They returned to find all six of the men dead from the same illness that had claimed the lives of the previous crewmen. Working around the bodies not wanting to disturb them, the three remaining crewmen constructed a door and a pulley from the inside of the cave using the wood from the life boats as Klaus had planned. The door was heavy but using the pulley and rope system they designed the weight was dispersed and it allowed the young boy to be able to lift and shut the door with ease. Klaus had noticed an opening high up above the main entrance to the cave. Standing on each other's shoulders, The Grief's older crewman with Klaus underneath struggled to stand straight while the young crewman stood atop them to attach a rope to a jagged rock just below it. Klaus ordered the boy to climb up and make the hole smaller, ensuring it was only big enough for him to fit through. Climbing up and down with a bag of mortar on his back made from mud and clay from the beach was back breaking slow work for him. The mortar was heavy on his shoulders and he had a few near misses climbing up and down the damp rope. It took the young crewman over a week to pack the mortar, making a tight smooth tunnel for him to crawl through. After six weeks, the men packed enough treasure to carry on horseback that would see them live comfortable lives if they didn't return. One last time they had the boy test the pulley on the door, it worked perfectly. They knew if anyone discovered the door they'd have a hard time figuring out it opened from behind. The boy closed the heavy door and pulled his way up the rope to the small exit high above. He was no stranger to scaling ropes after working on a ship. As he pulled himself out the men hadn't thought how the boy would get down on the outside. Klaus climbed onto the crewman's shoulders once more, signalling for the boy to drop his feet down toward Klaus. Hanging from the mouth of the small opening by his fingertips he held his breath as he struggled to lower his legs without losing his grip. He heard Klaus' calls from below but in a panic to climb back up he slipped and fell fast to the floor. His body smashed into the rocky ground and he felt his legs buckle under his weight, he passed out instantly from the pain and shock.

Klaus had never felt so guilty, he blamed himself for the boy's injuries. He secured him to his horse using the last of the rope they had left. Klaus hoped he could leave the boy somewhere to recover before he made his long journey home. He would make sure he topped up his purse with a few more of his coins. Klaus hoped that if he recovered, he could build a life for himself in Britain. He stood in the mouth of the cave and took one last look at the heavy door before turning away and walking through the waterfall for the last time.

Two hundred and forty years later, Madeline Wolf stood staring at the front of the door while Dominik and Dutch busied themselves in the cave. They had begun to start securing spotlights ready for Dutch to insert climbing pitons into the cave wall. Madeline smoothed her hand across the aged solid timber door, feeling the grain underneath her fingertips, her heart beating with excitement. She was desperate to gain entrance into the caves and see what treasures Klaus had left there for her to reclaim. But she was also annoyed, the unfortunate business with the landlord had forced her to pull her plans forward and now rush the job ahead of schedule. She wasn't a woman who liked to be rushed, she would always meticulously plan her events to run like clockwork. But now the clock was ticking, she knew she had only twenty-four hours before the police would start investigating the local businessman who had been reported missing and that it would lead them to the body shop to ask questions. She wondered why the fool of a man decided to stick his nose into her business, he had his money, he should have been happy with it. Madeline pondered the incident with the young girl at the petrol station and wondered if it had triggered his curiosity.

'I don't care about the details Dominik but are you sure they won't find the van anytime soon?' Madeline barked, Dominik stopped adjusting a spotlight and focussed his attention solely on her.

'Madame we took care of it, we filled the van full of concrete blocks and left the windows open before pushing it into the lake. Unless they use divers and why would they have any reason to? They won't find him anytime soon.'

'Him?' she said quietly in a whisper.

Suddenly Madeline felt hollow knowing her journey had taken a dark path, cold and calculating as she was, she was now an accomplice to murder and there was no turning back. She was used to getting what she wanted at any cost, but now that a life had been taken in the name of her private quest she realised she wasn't as malevolent as her external persona let on. She looked at the door, once more desperate to know what it concealed, she swallowed her emotions and knew she wouldn't let anything get in her way. It was only a matter of time before they gained entrance into the caves and she would be forced to correct her story to Dominik and Dutch, after not being fully forthcoming with the truth of what the cave contained. Written in Klaus' notes was a severe warning to not enter, as the risk of death was far too great. She glanced down at her aunt's diamond encrusted Rolex and back at the cave door. She was willing to take the risk.

'Get a move on you two, we haven't got much time.' she said callously.

CHAPTER SEVEN
TAKING A RISK

Georgie had been awake for an hour. She was eating her breakfast while watching 'Going Live!' laughing at her favourite comedy duo Trev and Simon and their silly on-screen antics. Georgie's mum had always been an early riser and would have normally watched Saturday morning television with her. Georgie missed her mum the most during these quiet times and hated sitting on a huge empty sofa alone. Sometimes she wished she had a younger brother or sister to laugh or squabble with, but that was something Georgie would never get to experience. Occasionally she stood up and glanced out of her front window over to Elliot's house, she was trying to see if the curtains had been opened. It was half past eight and Georgie was already eager to get outside and continue exploring Northshore. Although, it looked very much as though the Cassley's didn't rise too early on Saturday mornings. Feeling impatient and full of energy she rinsed her cereal bowl and placed it in the sink, trying not to make too much noise as her dad was still asleep upstairs. She knew he could do with the rest after the move and all the unpacking. She grabbed an unopened letter of her dad's off the kitchen table, along with a ballpoint pen and wrote a note on the back of it for him - 'Dad, gone out to explore for a bit. Will be back for lunch, Georgie x.'

She placed the note on the bottom step of the stairs so she knew he'd see it, grabbed her jacket off the coat rail and headed out of the house quietly closing the door behind her. Thomas had given her a set of keys on a mini carabiner keyring.

One for the garage and one for the back door, which she attached to a belt loop on her jeans after unlocking the garage door. Her BMX was covered in a fine dust from the previous day's ride out with Elliot. She was tempted to hook up the hose pipe to the external tap to clean the bike, when she heard Chinook's loud bark from across the street. It was a cold fresh morning with a little haze in the air and there was a thin layer of dew over the cars and front garden. Georgie wiped her finger along the top of her dad's car leaving a finger trail in the water as she quickly walked past it.

Chinook was patiently standing behind the gate at the end of Elliot's driveway staring at Georgie wagging his tail furiously, happy to see Elliot's new friend. Georgie crossed to see him and in doing so saw Elliot opening the living room curtains, they both waved excitedly, and Elliot ran to meet Georgie outside with Chinook.

'Hey! How's your leg today, is it any better?' Elliot asked.

'Yeah it's fine, bit of a bruise but not as sore today.'

Georgie appreciated Elliot's concern and realised she'd never experienced such empathy with her previous friends, they were always too self-centred to care about anyone else.

'I've got to pop to the shop for my mum, we've run out of potatoes and carrots of all things. She wondered if you and your dad would like to come over for tea with us tonight? She's making a cottage pie, it's not that bad either!' Elliot was hoping Georgie would accept, any reason for them to spend more time together was okay by him.

'Sure! My dad would like that, I'll ask him when we get back, he's still in bed. Lemme just lock up the garage and I'll come with you to the shop.'

Georgie ran over to her house while Elliot attached Chinook's lead to his studded collar. Chinook would stay with him off the lead, but Elliot knew it made people feel safer being around the big dog. Elliot walked across the road and met with Georgie as they started to walk towards town.

Station Street was a typical Welsh road, long and straight with two long rows of terraced houses built parallel to each other on opposite sides. The residents had personalised the front of their houses by painting their doors and window surrounds different colours, giving the houses their own sense of character. Georgie was happily taking in the different sounds coming from the houses. Many of the families who lived in them were now starting to make their houses come alive with activity, she could hear conversations, arguments, singing and even people cooking fry ups for their breakfast. One house had the front door wide open while a middle-aged lady wearing an apron hoovered the rug in the hallway. She smiled at them as they skipped past her house. On the opposite side of the street a boy no older than eighteen was struggling to install a new car stereo into his clapped-out Renault 5. As he attached the connecting wires he didn't realise the stereo was already turned on, or that it was turned up to full volume. Georgie watched him leap out of his chair as the latest New Kids on the Block hit 'You Got It' started blaring out of his speakers. Wearing an AC/DC t-shirt and having long black hair, he obviously wasn't a fan of popular chart music especially a boy band and looked instantly embarrassed. Georgie was surprised by how many residents left their front doors wide open and that the neighbours would just pop their heads into a doorway call out a 'hello' followed by a name and just wander into someone else's house. It was so odd to her that everyone seemed to know... everyone. As they reached the bottom of the street a man's legs were poking out from under his mustard yellow Vauxhall Chevette. Georgie and Elliot casually stepped over them as they were draped across half of the pavement. The postman shouted as he approached the car, 'How do Nige!' and the legs responded, 'Aye good Dai!' The community in Northshore was a lot more relaxed and friendlier than Georgie was used to, living so close to big towns like Cheltenham and Gloucester for most of her life. Northshore was certainly a refreshing eye opener for her.

As they approached the town's centre many of the shops were already open, including the butchers, newsagents, hairdressers and greengrocers. Standing outside of the newsagents were Dillon Davies and Carl Coombes, Carl clocked Georgie and Elliot and a look of glee appeared across his face as he nudged Dillon on the arm for his attention. Happily, in their own little world talking about their BMX stunts from the night before, they hadn't noticed the two bullies on the opposite side of the street. Elliot left Chinook outside the greengrocers secured to the drain pipe as he and Georgie went in to pick up the supplies for his mum. The greengrocers didn't just sell fruit and veg, they were also the town's florist and Georgie decided to pick up a bunch of tulips for Elliot's mum as a thank you for inviting her and her dad over for dinner. After swiftly buying their supplies they walked out of the greengrocers to find that Dillon and Carl were loitering outside by the wall, keeping their distance from Chinook.

'Alright Toady!' Carl shouted smirking at Elliot.

'Still here are you ginge?!' added Dillon maliciously, aimed at Georgie.

Elliot stopped in his tracks, amazed that after making fools of these two jokers in front of the whole class that they hadn't learned anything and still wanted to cause trouble. Elliot discreetly loosened Chinook from the drain pipe as the two boys walked up to Georgie and Elliot trying to look confident and threatening.

'We ain't going to forget your little book trick Toady, Tuesday after school you're having it!' Dillon hissed with a venomous snarl to his delivery. He meant every word and Elliot knew it.

'Yeah you and ginger nut here better look out, we saw you running home from school yesterday, we're not fools.' Carl's threat came across less threatening but that was his style.

Elliot stared at the two boys while holding a large bag of potatoes, he looked them both in the eye for a moment, shrugged his shoulders, then turned around and walked away. This enraged the two boys especially Dillon who grabbed a satsuma off the front display of the shop and threw it at Elliot missing him by an inch and hitting Georgie's tulips instead, damaging the petals.

'Hey!' Georgie shouted, she was about to charge at the bullies who were laughing hysterically when Elliot stopped her.

'No, wait a sec.' Elliot turned back to face the boys and placed his bag of potatoes on the floor next to his feet.

The boys started making fun of his shopping, calling him silly names like 'potato boy' and began to challenge him verbally.

'Come on then Toady what you going to do this time?' Carl heckled.

'Chinook heal...' Elliot commanded his bear sized dog to stand at his side, pointing to the floor next to his feet. Carl and Dillon hadn't anticipated the giant German Shepherd was so well trained. Chinook was already alert and immediately stood next to Elliot and dipped his head as if ready to attack, glaring at the two boys in front of him. Dillon and Carl were suddenly both less vocal but still stood their ground trying to look brave in the face of what was quickly starting to look like a dangerous dog.

'What's your stupid dog gonna do Toady? Lick us to death?!' they both started laughing, feeding off each other's immature humour.

'No, I'm just going to command him to bite and claw you.' Elliot said quite calmly, holding his hand just in front of Chinook's eyes.

The boys now stopped laughing and took notice of Elliot and how serious he looked.

'Hey c'mon mate we're only messing about, don't be so serious. He wouldn't do that, would he? Good dog … good dog.' Carl said starting to ponder the possibility that Elliot was telling the truth.

Elliot still steadily held his hand in front of Chinook's eyes then without warning he dropped it shouting the command 'Sic 'em boy! Sic 'em!'

Chinook turned ferocious, his nose widened, and his canines were exposed as he started snarling and barking, powerfully spraying his saliva over the pavement, terrifying the two bullies. His body was lurching forward as if he was getting ready to pounce. Carl and Dillon screamed and ran as fast as they could across the road, almost getting run over by a milk float that was returning to base in the process.

Elliot chuckled as he watched the boys now on the opposite side of the road continue to run away, in fear of being attacked by his dog. Georgie was impressed but also a little scared too, Chinook really played the guard dog role well, almost too well. Elliot clapped his hands together and Chinook snapped out of his guard dog role, returning back to wagging his tail. Elliot noticed Georgie looked uneasy and reassured her that it was just a party trick he taught Chinook as a pup and that he wouldn't have actually attacked the boys. Looking at how quickly Chinook returned back to normal, Georgie could see this was the case and he was back to his happy self-straight away, nudging at her hand with his big wet nose wanting a fuss.

'Where did you get the phrase 'Sic 'em' from, that's gnarly' Georgie asked.

'I dunno, I think it was in a film or something. I did start with the order 'growl', but I modified it over time in case I ever needed it to sound more threatening. It sure works. I've done it a few times now, mainly back home in Cardiff, it was a little rough and ready out and about there in the parks sometimes, with big gangs of boys around.'

As they walked, Georgie noticed the town had a video store and convinced Elliot they should pop in and check out the new releases. Her dad had promised he would sign up and rent a movie for them to watch together on Sunday night, to make the most of their long weekend. Her favourite film of the summer was Indiana Jones and the Last Crusade, and she was desperate to watch it again, she was curious if it was available to rent. Chinook stood guard by the door as Elliot and Georgie perused the new release shelf. Looking around the shop, Georgie loved all the Hollywood posters that adorned the walls and noticed there was a small room attached that housed four arcade game systems. She wasn't really into arcade games and had always thought them a waste of money, but fancied giving them a go one day, just for the fun of it. Georgie couldn't find the film she was looking for on the shelves, so decided to ask the man behind the desk.

Ray was in his forties, overweight with a balding head, a thick moustache and always wore a t-shirt easily two sizes too small for him with 'Acorn Video' emblazoned across the front. He had owned the store since it opened six years prior and he was the equivalent of a rock star in Northshore. Supplying the local residents with the latest Hollywood blockbusters in the comfort of their own home at just £1.25 a pop. Georgie approached the counter just as Ray finished rewinding one of his rental tapes in a VHS machine before placing it back in its case. He noticed Georgie approach the desk and started to speak.

'Takes no effort to rewind a tape, that's a twenty pence fine on their account now. What you after my love, need any help?' Georgie was used to her Welsh grandparents calling her 'love' but still found it a little bizarre that absolute strangers used it affectionately towards each other in South Wales, in common conversation. She found it quite comforting and sweet but couldn't ever imagine saying it herself to anyone.

'Hi, my dad said he'd sign up for a membership this weekend, we're new here. What does he need to do? Also, do you know when the new Indiana Jones movie is out to rent?' Georgie asked.

Ray sucked air in through his teeth as though someone had just kicked him in the shin and he pulled out a huge book from under his counter slamming it down on the surface. He spoke to himself as he read out the alphabetised pages and dates from the directory. He flicked through until he eventually hit the film he was looking for. He tapped his finger on the page targeting some text and made a clicking noise with his mouth that signalled a disappointing result, before turning the book around for Georgie to see.

'Still got bit of a wait sorry love, not out till February next year. We've got the first two though if you want either of those, Raiders is my favourite!' he pointed to the action section and Georgie made note. He reached behind him and pulled a membership form off the top of a stack of papers.

'Get your dad to fill this form in anyway and get him to bring it in with some ID, when you're ready then I'll get you all signed up! Come in end of Jan too and I'll put your name down for a copy on release day.'

'Okay thanks will do.' Georgie said.

After handing her the form, Ray then grabbed a pile of empty video cases that were stacked on the counter and lifted the wooden counter flap, walking out on to the shop floor to start refreshing the shelves with titles that had been returned. Georgie headed out of the video store with Elliot.

'He's funny that guy, he asked my mum out on a date a few weeks back, she got so embarrassed! He still gives her two rentals for the price of one, even though she turned him down. Poor guy.'

Elliot laughed with Georgie, he hadn't laughed so much in the last few months and he was enjoying flexing his cheek muscles.

The pair walked back up towards Station Street from the town centre, inspired by the video store and chatting about what their favourite movies were and what music they liked, agreeing on most of them. They approached the entrance to the lane that Elliot had taken Georgie the night before on their BMX's. Georgie glanced down the lane as they crossed it and noticed the black Land Rover she had encountered at the petrol station, parked no more than a hundred meters away with its engine ticking over. She grabbed Elliot's arm immediately and pulled him back behind a garden wall to hide. Chinook sat tilting his head looking at them confused in the middle of the lane. Elliot quickly called him to his side to stand still and out of sight. Georgie explained to Elliot that they were the people she had the nasty encounter with the day before and that they were renting one of her dad's friends' buildings.

'It's them El, down there the black 4x4.' she said whispering.

Elliot leaned out to look down the lane and saw the expensive car. 'Nice wheels' he said.

'I don't trust them. Simon's van was down there last night, I thought my dad must have told him about the accident at the garage and he went to have a word, but my dad hadn't spoken to him.' Georgie said.

'Maybe he had a call out or something? Wonder why they're just parked in the middle of the lane?' Elliot replied, trying to peer around the wall again without being seen.

'I don't know, Simon told us he had a night planned in with his family, he shouldn't have been there last night. I hope he's okay, I don't want to be the cause for someone else getting hurt.'

Both Georgie and Elliot stretched their heads around the wall trying to spy on the black 4x4. Nothing seemed to be happening, the car wasn't moving, and nobody was getting in or out. Then finally the brake lights dimmed, and the Land Rover pulled forward revealing Carl Coombes and Dillon Davies standing by the side of it.

'Wonder why they were they talking to those dummies? I bet they were telling them off for something' Elliot said.

'No idea.' Georgie replied, she looked back down at the boys then at Elliot 'Let's go ask them.'

When the Land Rover was out of sight Georgie and Elliot walked out from behind the wall and headed down the lane toward Carl and Dillon. Both boys looked a little lost and almost looked relieved to see Elliot and Georgie walking towards them, which seemed strange considering how Elliot had only recently frightened them with Chinook.

'Keep that dog away from me Toady. I'll tell the police!' Dillon yelled.

'You keep calling me Toady and maybe I won't!'

Georgie intervened looking at Elliot to calm him down, then back at Dillon with a disappointed look on her face.

'Stop calling him that … and stop calling me stuff too, it makes you both look stupid.' Georgie said to the boys.

Dillon looked at the ground as though he had just been told off by his mother.

'What did those men in the Land Rover want, what did they say to you?'. Georgie demanded.

Dillon looked at Carl and they both started to walk up the lane toward the road ignoring Georgie. Georgie rolled her eyes and knew she wasn't going to get anything out of them, so turned the other way to follow where the car had gone. Carl glanced over his shoulder and saw what Georgie was doing, he stopped walking and called after her.

'Oi Carrot, don't follow them!' Georgie stopped and replied back to Carl 'Don't call me that, why shouldn't I follow them?!'.

Carl slowly walked back towards Georgie and Elliot, the gravel of the lane crunching under his trainers as he walked.

'Look, they're bad news. Some weird French guy and a bodybuilder, they were stinking dirty too, absolutely covered in mud. I know we like to cause trouble for a laugh, but we know serious trouble when we see it. They were trying to get us to go with them somewhere. They didn't say where, but they offered us a hundred pound to share between us and asked if we were any good at climbing.'

Georgie and Elliot were now intrigued, and Elliot joined in the conversation.

'Climbing? That's a bit specific… and a hundred pounds, are you sure that's what they said? Don't bad guys normally offer kids … sweets?'

'Yeah, they said if we went with them and helped them climb to open a door or something where they were struggling to fit, they'd give us a hundred quid then drop us back off here later. They looked well dodgy though, so I said our mum was waiting for us up the lane. They got annoyed and drove off, they seem to be in a hurry whatever it is.' Carl said.

As much as Elliot agreed to stay away from the men in the Land Rover, he still couldn't understand why the two boys were both in Northshore that morning.

'Why are you back in Northshore Carl? It's Saturday, there's no school today, don't you both live in Sambrook Bay, or somewhere a few miles away?'

'My Nan lives up the road, we stayed here last night. Anyway, my dad's picking us up soon, we're going to the football in Cardiff.' Carl had had enough of chatting and wanted to get away, but before he made the effort to walk away he spoke up once more.

'I don't particularly like either of you losers but do yourselves a favour and stay away from those guys. I'm telling you, they're bad news.'

With his last words of cautious advice, Carl and Dillon retreated back up the lane and disappeared onto the main road. Elliot could tell Georgie's curiosities had been piqued, she peered down the lane towards the direction of the Land Rover, then glanced at her watch. It was nearly ten o'clock, her dad would be up and awake by now and Elliot needed to get his mum's shopping to her ASAP before he got in trouble.

'El, I've got an idea.' she said.

Elliot stood there, his arms starting to ache slightly from the weight of the potatoes knowing what Georgie was about to suggest.

'Will we need the bikes?' he asked with his eyebrows raised.

'Absolutely.' she replied.

Georgie was nearly out of breath after running back to the house and her fingers ached from carrying the bag of carrots for Elliot. The pink tulips she bought were looking a little worse for wear. She managed to smooth them back into shape before filling a pint glass with water, plonking them in and putting them on the kitchen window sill. Thomas Rivers was still in his dressing gown reading the newspaper in the living room, he heard Georgie come in and faintly heard a 'Hi Dad' as she hurried upstairs. After changing into her old jeans and trainers Georgie was storming back downstairs to be greeted by her dad standing at the bottom of the stairs.

'Hey there what's the hurry!' he said, as she steadied herself with her hands on his shoulders, after coming down the stairs far quicker than she meant to.

'Sorry Dad, going out with Elliot on our bikes again. Just need to be quick to get back for lunch that's all. You okay?'

'I'm fine sweetheart, are you sure you're okay? You seem a bit… edgy?' he said concerned.

Georgie took in a few slow deep breaths and tried to calm down to not make her adrenaline give away her plans, or that she was hiding something.

'I'm good, just in a rush, Elliot's waiting. Actually, Dad, could you help me tighten my handlebars before I go?'

'Of course, as long as you're okay. You'd tell me if something was up right?'

'Yeah you know I would. We're just going riding Dad, it's fine.' Georgie said, trying to remain composed and calm in front of her suspecting parent.

As calm as Georgie thought she was being Thomas knew something was up but chose to let her decide if she was going to share with him any information. They went outside, and Thomas held Georgie's front wheel in between his knees as he tightened the headset of her handlebars. Elliot was waiting at the gate along with Chinook as Georgie put on her helmet and hopped onto her bike. Her dad held the gate open for her to ride straight out saying 'Hello' to Elliot at the same time, when Georgie suddenly remembered about their invitation. Doubling back on her bike towards her house she called out.

'Dad! I forgot to ask. Elliot's mum invited us over for dinner tonight and I said yes! See you soon!'

Thomas shook his head and laughed to himself as he waved watching the two new friends cycle off together, with Chinook running faithfully behind. As happy as he was to see Georgie having fun, his intuition was telling him that something wasn't quite right.

Georgie loved the feeling of cool air on her face as she rode fast downhill, almost making her eyes water. She knew going this fast was dangerous and she that could lose control of the bike at any moment. It was exciting and risky, and she got a huge kick out of it. Elliot took the lead and pulled off a skid to turn down into the gravelly lane that led to where they saw the Land Rover. Georgie had a plan to split up and she headed straight past the turning and instead headed for the front of the old body shop via the opposite entrance to the lane just off the main road to see if they had parked there. With Chinook at his side Elliot eased off his speed letting his BMX come to a gradual stop, rather than kicking up excessive dust from pulling on the brakes in the lane. Georgie was now passing the front of the body shop, realising there was no sign of the Land Rover, she doubled back to access the lane from the opposite end to Elliot from around the back.

Chinook was panting after all the running and found a nearby puddle of rain water to lap at, needing a refresh. Elliot sat on the saddle of his bike using his feet on the ground to inch himself forward trying to not be exposed at the back of the unit. As he scanned the rear car park through the heavy steel gates he could see the 4x4 was parked at the old unit, but there was no sign of the men that Georgie had described. He started to wonder if they had gone elsewhere for the day. Georgie had now reached the section of back lane that was in close proximity to the back entrance where she saw Simon Jenkins' Van the night before. This time the steel gates were shut, and Elliot was there peering through, looking for any movement inside.

As Georgie approached, Elliot suddenly raised his hand waving for her to stop. The large man Georgie had described to Elliot had come outside, with what looked like a heavy kit bag. He was easily loading it into the boot of the black 4x4. Elliot was shocked at the sheer size of the man's arms, especially when he was lifting the bag into the car. He had never seen a man this powerful looking in real life before. Elliot wouldn't admit it, but the man frightened him. He imagined just one of the man's hands were big enough to grab his entire head and lift him off the ground with ease. Elliot pulled out a walkie-talkie from inside his jacket and pointed at it to Georgie. Elliot had given her the sister walkie-talkie just as they were out of their estate. Georgie switched hers on and turned the volume down low. Through the static noise of the cheap Fisher Price walkie-talkies that Elliot received for Christmas years before, Georgie could just about make out what Elliot was saying.

He told her to stay where she was, as there was a man in the carpark. The huge man went back into the body shop after loading up the boot and Elliot signalled Georgie over to him.

Unbeknown to them Dominik was observing them from the top window, he was pondering how best to utilise this golden opportunity. Dutch was sweating as he arrived in the upstairs office, where he noticed Dominik hiding behind a curtain spying on something outside.

'You are a truly bizarre man. What are you doing, there's loads to do?' Dutch asked confused.

'There's two kids down by the back gate snooping around. I caught the reflection from one of their helmets and I've been watching them. Look there they are, two dirty little spies.' Dominik said pointing, sounding tired from working through the night. Dutch grabbed Dominik by the shoulder and moved him to one side, allowing him the space to hide behind the curtain. He also began to analyse the two children looking into the carpark from the lane.

'Do you reckon it's the boys we approached earlier?' Dutch said.

'No, one of them has long red hair. I think it's the girl who knocked me over yesterday and I think they're spying on us.'

Pondering Dominik's theory he looked back out of the window hoping to get a clear view of the two children down on the ground. Georgie and Elliot were growing impatient and Georgie suggested they both double back and wait out front, so they could look less conspicuous. Meanwhile back in the office, Dutch and Dominik were hatching a plan of their own.

'I have an idea that may just work to our advantage here Dutch, let's slightly change our plan and take half the equipment back to the cave now. I have a feeling we can lay a trap with these little brats.'

Dutch finished changing out of his sodden clothes and looked seriously at Dominik, 'I'm listening.'

Back out on the main road Georgie and Elliot sat on their bikes at the side of the pavement away from the entrance to the lane and the body shop. Chinook sat loyally next to Elliot waiting for them to move again.

'What do you think they've got in that bag? That guy's a monster as well, is he the one you knocked over?'

'No, it was the smaller French guy, he's got his leg in plaster. I've got no idea what's in the bag, but they're obviously planning something.'

As Georgie finished her sentence Elliot saw behind her the black Land Rover Defender had appeared at the junction waiting to pull out into the road.

'Georgie get down!' he shouted, and he held Chinook by the collar not to give them away.

They both crouched down behind a parked car and tried to look at the Land Rover as best as they could through the parked car windows.

'They're going somewhere, what should we do?' Elliot said.

'Let them pull away and we'll try and follow them, see where they go.' Georgie replied.

The Land Rover pulled out and steadily drove away, heading out from the town centre. Georgie stood up and straightened out her bike, aiming it in the direction of the black Defender. Elliot had a moment of realisation and thought they may be asking for trouble following the men.

'Georgie should we just call the police on them? I don't want either of us getting kidnapped or anything. Carl Coombes is a real idiot and even he said to stay away from them!'

'I agree, but let's try and track them for now, we won't get too close. We'll need to have something on them before we can call the police, otherwise they won't want to know! Let's just try and find out where they're going with that equipment.'

Elliot reluctantly agreed and let Georgie take the lead. Georgie's heart was racing as she pedalled in pursuit of the two dangerous men.

CHAPTER EIGHT
IN PURSUIT OF DANGER

Dutch kept a close eye on the speedometer, driving slightly under the speed limit and allowing every traffic light to hit red causing them to stop as frequently as possible. Through his tinted aviator Ray Bans he kept checking in his rear-view mirror, ensuring he caught a glimpse of the two young bikers following in the distance behind. He had to ensure that he went fast enough not to arise suspicion, but slow enough that his followers could keep them in sight. The roads were still a little wet from rainfall overnight, but the weather was now dry and clear with bright white skies overhead. Dutch was looking forward to returning to the California sun once this job was over, he tired of how wet and miserable the United Kingdom was during the winter months and yearned for the deep blue skies of America. He watched as the two kids that followed weaved in and out of parked cars and even cycled on the pavement cautiously trying not to be seen. But they hadn't accounted for Dutch's years of military experience and security training. For Dutch, this literally was child's play. He'd seen his fair share of conflict. After a heavily armed battle by air and land, Iraq had invaded Iran in late 1980. This Created work opportunities for ex-military security like Dutch and he took full advantage of it. For three months during the summer of 1981 he was stationed as the private bodyguard for an Iraqi government official, who was based in Iran. Through the infernal heat and dust on Iran's roads, Dutch had gained a talent for driving while keeping one eye on the road and the other in his mirrors. Being knee deep in a conflict zone, Dutch took the money and ran before Iran regained its territories a year later. Two years prior he had helped the British military in Operation Banner, acting as hired driver security for the visiting English MPs during the Northern Ireland conflict. However, he grew tired of having to check under his vehicle with a mirror taped to a golf iron to locate any bombs that had been potentially placed there. Dutch preferred to be in control, warzones offered little of that comfort. Dutch and driving however went together like eggs and bacon, he was as precise manoeuvring a vehicle under pressure as he was reverse parking a Mini Metro into the space of a double decker bus.

This was an easy game for him and he believed in the plan that Dominik had cooked up back at the unit but unlike Dominik, Dutch had rules. He had now discovered that Dominik was a step below a full-blown psychopath and a cold-blooded killer after the intrusion from the landlord. As little as these kids meant to him, he promised himself he wouldn't allow Dominik the freedom to seriously hurt them. Rough them up a bit maybe, scare them yes, but he'd pull the plug if he saw the venom start to appear in Dominik's eyes.

Georgie was starting to get a little nervous, she hadn't anticipated how far out of town the Land Rover would go. They had tailed the black Defender for fifteen minutes before she slowed down and signalled for Elliot to stop. Her legs were aching, and she was feeling the strain of the BMX's fixed single gear, Chinook was panting heavily also, needing a break. Luckily for Georgie there had been very few hills to contend with in Northshore, mainly having to cycle on the flat. Elliot pulled up alongside Georgie on the curb as they watched the Land Rover from afar taking the road toward the beach. Georgie was trying to get her bearings, luckily for her there was only one road in and one road out of Northshore.

'They're heading for the beach. That roads a dead end so we can hold back a minute and take our time. The furthest they can go is the car park below the cliffs.' Elliot said.

Georgie looked out towards the ocean, the sea sparkling in the morning sunshine was a beautiful sight to behold. Her eyes swept across the coastline and fell on the cliffs that fronted it. Puzzled, Georgie wondered why they had headed toward the beach and started to wonder if they were using the equipment to dig. She remembered her dad's conversation with Simon Jenkins at the café, where he mentioned someone had discovered two million pounds worth of roman artefacts close to the beach. Maybe they'd hit the jackpot she thought? But judging by their set up it seemed more than just the usual amateur metal detector and shovels. They had professional and expensive heavy-duty gear in those bags and there had been no whispers of a new discovery around the town. After catching their breath Georgie and Elliot carefully navigated the road over to the junction that led down to the beach. During the summer months the road would naturally be a lot busier with local residents and visitors from further afield, making the most of the beach and the summer weather. But today in mid-November it was eerily quiet, Georgie and Elliot stopped in the middle of the road, contemplating their next move. From this point on they would be more exposed. There were little to no trees decorating the side of the road and the beach opened out with only the cliffs offering any shelter. Georgie and Elliot would be easily spotted from the car park, they had to be careful and take their time not to be noticed by the men.

Dominik was growing impatient as they sat in the car park with the diesel engine ticking over. His plan of luring them to the caves wouldn't pan out if the kids had lost interest and turned back to the town centre. He assumed they weren't as brave as they initially appeared, which he was finding disappointing to accept. He tapped on the armrest impatiently and kept turning his head to look behind them.

'You keep doing that and they won't follow,' Dutch said calmly, keeping his head forward but his eyes firmly locked on the rear-view mirror, 'Just keep looking forward, I've got this.'

Dominik sighed as he turned his head forward and started tapping his foot in the foot well. Dutch sat still, quietly concentrating his attention on the entrance of the car park, the only way the two kids could go if they were still in pursuit. With electric fences lining the road to keep the farmer's sheep in their fields, Georgie's idea of bypassing the road was out of the question. Elliot had got caught on one of the fences in the past and warned Georgie away from them as he didn't fancy getting any electric shocks either. Georgie had to think fast, at that moment an old lime green Volkswagen camper van with two surfboards strapped to its roof rack turned into the road causing Georgie and Elliot to move out of the way. Georgie saw her opportunity, they could ride alongside the van and get to the bottom of the cliffs without being seen. Georgie called out to Elliot.

'El, I've got an idea, ride next to the van we'll use it as cover!'

Elliot instantly understood and threw a confident thumbs up. He thought they'd struggle, trying to time their peddling with the van. But luckily, the driver didn't seem in any hurry or that the camper van couldn't manage too high a speed giving its old condition.

Dutch noticed movement in his mirror and could see the surf boards and top half of the van with ease, he kept a close eye on it as it approached and as the van entered the car park he caught a glimpse of a bicycle tyre disappear at the back of the van behind the base of the cliff.

'We're in business,' he said.

Dominik quickly thrust his head around expecting to see the two youngsters behind them.

'What do you mean? It's just surfers in a van!'

'Trust me, they're still with us,' Dutch replied coolly.

Hiding tight against the rocks, Georgie and Elliot positioned themselves to get a closer look of the Land Rover. The two surfers hadn't wasted any time unloading their van as they ran past Georgie and Elliot paying them no attention. Silly kids playing silly games they most probably thought. As Georgie inched her face out from behind the cliff wall just enough to use one eye to spy on the men, she saw that the 4x4 was now on the move. The car park was quite makeshift, a field which had been separated from access to the cliff tops by a now years old wooden fence with one stone wall running along one side. Georgie could see the big man jump out of the car and watched him remove the rails from one section of the fence putting them down on the floor, he got back into the Land Rover and after driving through the gap he got back out and replaced the two heavy looking fence pieces, looking around to see he wasn't noticed. They now had access to the entire cliff area and Georgie watched with amazement as the Land Rover disappeared up high onto the fields above the cliffs.

'What are they doing?' Elliot asked.

'No wonder they've got a 4x4, they've just removed part of the fence and driven through! I can't see them now we'll have to get closer.' she said exited.

Georgie moved out into the open and cycled over to the car park just in time to see the tail end of the Land Rover disappear up over the hilltop, Elliot couldn't believe what he was seeing.

'You're not allowed to drive up there it's dangerous, it leads to the cliffs!' he said amazed.

'They must have found something El, whatever it is they're not wanting the authorities or council to know about it, otherwise it would be cordoned off and you'd have a professional crew here investigating. I'm guessing they'll be pretty easy to spot if we went up there after them?'

'Yes easily, but let's take a different route, where they're heading you can access it from the garden ruins on the far side as well. That way they won't see us.'

As Georgie and Elliot ran pushing their bikes, Elliot filled in Georgie on some local history that he had been taught in school. He had learned that in the 1600's a large Manor House was constructed on the cliffs of Northshore bay, it was so large the local residents referred to it as Northshore Castle. It was built by the towns wealthiest lord, Sir Edward North who left the building to his descendants who were residents there until its demolition in the 1960's. The building had become too expensive and unstable to maintain and after it served as a hospital for returning soldiers from World War Two the local council sent in the bulldozers. All that was left of the once great monument was its gardens and the crumbled foundations around it. As Georgie approached the garden walls she tried to envisage what it must have been like and tried to picture the grand building as Elliot described. Scrambling through the gardens they exited out through a gate almost directly onto the edge of the highest cliff. Georgie was amazed by the view and shocked at the sheer drop in front of her. It hadn't felt like they had climbed as high as they were and so quickly, it nearly took her breath away.

'These bikes are slowing us down. I tell you what it's dead quiet here this morning, let's hide them in these bushes no one will think to look for them. We'll be less visible then too, we can stay low to the grass.' Elliot said.

Georgie knew Elliot was right, but she struggled with the idea of parting with her precious bike. Reluctantly she agreed, but only after they had managed to convincingly conceal the bikes amongst the foliage.

They followed the path of the cliff face doubling back on themselves away from the gardens. The wind was noticeably stronger being exposed so high up and close to the cliff face and Georgie could feel the force of the wind trying to take her feet from under her. In a matter of minutes, they saw the roof of the black Land Rover up ahead, parked dangerously close to the edge of the cliff with the boot wide open. Elliot signalled for Georgie to drop down low and they both fell into a commando crawl. Lying on the ground and peering through the thick grass, Georgie studied the area and noticed the men were nowhere to be seen.

'Where are they? I don't see them,' she said.

Elliot squinted, scanning around focussing near the Land Rover when out of the corner of his eye he saw the large man return to the vehicle. Elliot nudged Georgie with his elbow and they both watched the man toss an empty kit bag into the back of the car slamming the boot shut. Not far behind hobbling on crutches, struggling to navigate so close to the cliff edge the smaller man appeared and climbed into the car. The men appeared to be arguing as they closed the doors of the Defender before the car wheel-spun away churning up chunks of grass and soil. Georgie and Elliot watched them head back in the direction of the car park and knew they had to investigate.

'We need to get down there, it looks like they've made a path down the side of the rock face.' Georgie said intrigued.

'I was afraid you'd say that.' Elliot leapt up off the ground and started running towards the edge of the cliff, Chinook running ahead of him thinking it was a race. Georgie smiled watching them run, before leaping up to chase after them.

As they arrived at the cliff edge Georgie was proven correct. There was a wall of bushes on the edge of the cliff that had been cleared away, making an opening of around two meters. This was only really noticeable up close; most people didn't walk this near to the edge so would have happily walked past not noticing it from a slight distance. Looking through the gap and noticing the drop below, Georgie realised there was a natural ledge leading across the cliff face. But it was dangerously narrow. A fall from this height would lead to certain death. Georgie with her climbing experience and little to no fear of heights thought nothing of the sheer drop to the ocean and rocks below. To Elliot's surprise she stepped down off the grass verge onto the rock face below, stepping onto its natural ledge. Standing on a platform no wider than her shoulders, she looked along the cliff face heading away from her. In the distance she could see a small waterfall. Looking ahead, Georgie soon realised that at certain points heading towards the waterfall, wall anchors had been installed into the cliff face and a long rope had been thread through to provide a safety harness for whoever had been using the ledge. She wondered if the larger of the men had installed them, he looked as though he was comfortable or at least experienced in outdoor activities. He may have even been ex-military she thought. Elliot slowly lowered himself down onto the ledge and he felt the world start to spin, Georgie called out his name and put her hand on his shoulder to steady his nerves.

'It's okay, you're okay El. I used to feel giddy too when I started climbing high with Dad. Just keep your eyes on me and hold onto this.'
Georgie guided Elliot's hand toward the rope and as soon as he felt secure his heart rate slowed and he could feel himself relax.

'Georgie, that's one heck of a drop. I'm not sure about this, Chinook you stay up there boy.'

'El it's fine, it's narrow here but look, the further you go along it widens out. By the time we get to that waterfall we can stand next to each other without needing the rope. C'mon it's only about fifteen meters, follow me and go slow, keep a tight grip on the rope. These anchors aren't going anywhere, they look solid as a rock.'

Georgie tugged at the rope causing Elliot to feel queasy. Georgie set off putting one hand in front of the other as she confidently scaled her way across the cliff front. Elliot slowly followed and as Georgie had said, the rope felt secure. No doubt about it the ledge did seem as though it was getting wider the closer they got to the waterfall. Elliot had managed to catch up with Georgie, and had a rhythm going overlapping his hands to ensure he never let go of the rope, if he accidentally did he at least had one hand gripping the rope.

Arriving at the front of the waterfall, Georgie looked in amazement at what was in front of her. The rope had led them here and they had even seen the two men climbing up from the cliff, but now they were faced with a dead end. A large ledge stood firm as the waterfall smashed water down onto it, covering it with a slippery layer of moss as the water escaped over either side of the platform. On the floor to the right of the waterfall, Georgie noticed a plastic bucket that had a pile of what looked like large wet sheets of folded plastic inside it. Looking back at the waterfall and then behind her to the dangerous drop below she knew she was missing something obvious. It couldn't be a dead end; the men came down here with a full kit bag and left with an empty one. They must have stashed the contents of the bag nearby, they hadn't gone to all that effort to throw the contents into the sea surely? The thick black plastic sheets meant something Georgie knew it, she walked over and picked one up. They were cut into a rectangle no larger than a typical bath towel and seemed freshly wet. Georgie stood there for a moment staring at the waterfall. She rolled up her sleeve, walked over and pushed her arm through the water. Cutting through slowly, expecting to feel the surface of the cliff wall behind it. Her arm disappeared into the freezing cold water, but her hand didn't meet any resistance. Georgie looked at Elliot, smiled and without thinking she threw the soft plastic sheet over her head and body and walked straight through the waterfall. Elliot was lost for words, he screamed 'Georgie!' at the top of his voice and couldn't quite understand what he had just seen. Before he had time to think, Georgie burst back through the waterfall wide eyed and hysterical.

'Get in here you have to see this! It's a hidden cave!' she bellowed.

Elliot quickly wrapped himself in one of the plastic sheets closed his eyes and charged straight through the waterfall.

Georgie and Elliot both stood in awe as they looked around the huge cave trying to take everything in. There were enormous stalactites hanging from the ceiling glistening in the light and there was a ten-foot opening looking out towards the sea forming a huge window allowing the afternoon light to flood in. Sitting on the floor just in front of them was a petrol generator that Elliot recognised. His dad used to use one similar when they went camping or on day trips to the motocross. Elliot knelt down primed the fuel into the carburettor and pulled hard on the pull cord igniting the small engine to life. Suddenly the cave came alive as spotlights illuminated the walls and the ceilings all around them. There was a surprising amount of equipment strewn around the cave. A makeshift kitchen next to a campfire with pots and pans, shovels and digging equipment including crowbars and pickaxes leant against the wall. There were even tripods set up that looked like they were waiting to have cameras placed on them. Georgie noticed the floodlights were mainly pointing in one direction and by the time her eyeline had followed them, she saw what they were aimed at. In front of them was what looked like a man-made wooden door, no taller than chest high to her and it looked as though it had been made to suit a naturally forming hole in the wall of the cave.

'What's this? It looks like it's been here for years,' Georgie said as she walked closer to the door pressing her hand against it.

It was firm, and she was surprised it didn't show any signs of rot, especially being in such a damp cave. As she brushed her hand across the door she noticed a hammer and yet more climbing pegs strewn along the floor next to her. She recognized them instantly from her climbing days out with her dad in the Peak District, they were very similar to the pitons that were used on the training site there. Looking up the wall next to the door she noticed the pitons had been installed leading up close to the ceiling of the cave.

'Elliot look, they're trying to get access to that opening high up there. There's no way that big guy would fit through it's too narrow… I bet that's why they were trying to convince Carl and Dillon to climb for them, they would have killed themselves trying to climb that.'

'I'd put my money on the skinny one getting that broken leg from trying to climb it himself too,' Elliot said.

'I reckon I could do it, it'd be easy for me, I'd get through there. But I'd need my climbing shoes and harness from the house.'

'Do you think they're trying to open this door?' Elliot kicked at the wooden door looking up at the small opening high above them. 'How does it open there's no handle or anything?' he said.

'They must know something, with all this equipment here, they're obviously being careful not to disturb the rock, otherwise they would have just used force to get through the door. I bet they think the door opens from behind somehow looking at it. I'd agree too, like you said there's no handles or anything on this side and it's not going anywhere.' Georgie pushed her shoulder up against the door, it seemed as solid as the rock around them and didn't budge.

'Maybe climbing up and going through that hole makes sense and look there's a cross painted just below it, it must mean something? This door ain't moving from out here that's for sure.' Georgie looked around the cave as if hoping to find an answer.

'I don't like this, I think we definitely need to call the police now.' Elliot looked worried, he'd felt uncomfortable following the men and now standing in this mysterious cave he wasn't sure he wanted any part of it. Georgie understood, as intrigued as she was she didn't want to get herself, or Elliot in any serious trouble. They had already risked enough as it was. But she couldn't help being curious of what was behind the door and even the cave itself felt magical to her. She took one last look around, desperately trying to find any clues to the nature of the door or what lay behind it. Whatever it was, these men were using everything available to them to gain entry, but something was obviously holding them back.

Elliot turned off the generator, the cave suddenly fell uncomfortably silent. The sound of the waves crashing at the cliff below and the waterfall were now very prominent. He picked up his water proof plastic sheet and draped it over his head holding it firm under his chin, standing at the pouring water he patiently waited to leave looking at Georgie. She took one last look through the large opening in the cliff face, looking out at the ocean and to the deathly drop below. She closed her eyes and her mum appeared in her thoughts, a memory of one of their last conversations together before she died. Georgie was back there now with the memory consuming her thoughts, she could hear her mother's words as if she was standing right next to her in the cave.

'If you believe in something in this world Georgie, don't let it slip you by. Grab it with both hands and embrace it. If you're not hurting anyone else in the process, you go for it.'

A single tear ran down Georgie's face, she missed her mother desperately and knew if she was still around, she wouldn't be standing in this cave at all. She'd still be living in Cheltenham going about her day to day life with her materialistic friends and trying desperately hard to fit in. In the little time she had known Elliot, she already knew he was going to be her best friend and torn as she was, she wasn't about to let her curiosities let him down. Georgie wiped away the tear, hoping Elliot wouldn't notice and faced him.

'C'mon let's get out of here,' she said.

Elliot was relieved as they both pushed their way back out through the waterfall, together.

After retrieving their BMX's from amongst the trees and making their way back to the road from the beach, Georgie and Elliot theorised what could be hiding behind the door in the cave and how it got there.

'Do you reckon aliens put it there?' Elliot asked, as they both threw their legs over their saddles ready to ride home.

'I honestly don't know, it could be anything. It's such an odd place to find a door!' Georgie set off and Elliot kept the pace next to her while they continued to chat, with Chinook darting in and out of the bikes.

'Maybe bigfoot is locked in there?!' Elliot said with a playful look on his face.

'Whatever it is El I'd say it's very important to those men. I think they must have known it was there all along, who would have thought to look down there in the first place, it doesn't make any sense?'

'So, do you think we should tell the police when we get back to town? Or stay quiet?'

'I'm not sure they'd believe us to be honest, plus we don't know if they've done anything illegal yet. It does look suspicious though. Maybe I'll ask my dad to chat to his old friend Simon first, see if he knows anything.'

As Georgie and Elliot made their way back towards the centre of Northshore, they were completely unaware of the black Land Rover professionally and accurately tailing them a few hundred yards behind. Dutch was chewing on a matchstick and was calm and focussed while Dominik ranted in anger.

'Filthy little rats, if they head to the police station I say we mow them down on the doorstep!'

'That's overreacting a little don't you think my friend? Let's not forget whose idea this was. The police wouldn't believe those kids anyway, even if they did we'd still have time on our side. The way the law works in this country, it's as slow as its rail lines.' Dutch tried to keep Dominik calm.

'Just keep on them, we can't lose them, or the plan won't work. Where is Madeline anyway? She'll want to be here when we open that door.' Dominik said

'She told me she was collecting something from the airport, more of her home essentials from Germany I'm assuming. I did offer to drive her there, but she wanted us to carry on here and get things prepped, so she took a cab.'

'No doubt she'll be on board, she's colder than the Jura Mountains in peak winter,' Dominik hissed.

Dutch removed his sunglasses and placed them in the centre console, the traffic lights were on amber and about to turn red up ahead, he could see the two children had stopped to wait at them. Holding back allowing cars to filter in front of them so not to be seen, he brought the Land Rover to a halt, knocked it out of gear and pulled up the hand brake. He turned to Dominik and leant over him reaching into the glove box. Dutch pulled out a Beretta M9 semi-automatic 9mm side arm, he checked the barrel was loaded and fed it into a holster attached to his shoulder.

'Don't you worry my friend, this will be a piece of cake.'

CHAPTER NINE
BREAKING AND ENTERING

Elliot's heart was still pounding as he opened the back door to his house, he could feel his pulse pumping deep in his chest and up into his throat. His mum was busy cooking in the kitchen and his little sister Alice was happily playing with her dolls on the dining room floor. Chinook starting barking at him and as soon as they walked into the house, he started scratching at the cupboard in the utility room that contained his food. It had been a busy morning of exploring for all three of them and Chinook needed refuelling. Elliot found it hard to talk to anyone straight away, as though he was keeping a secret that his life depended on. His mum had acknowledged his arrival with a loving 'Hello handsome', to which at first, he didn't respond. Not that she had expected a response as she was busy starting to mash the potatoes that Elliot had collected for her earlier in the morning. Now boiled, hot, white and fluffy, she added a generous dollop of butter and splashed some milk into the saucepan. Using a potato masher, she began to crush the boiled potatoes down into a soft mash. For a relatively small and slender woman, she didn't hold back when it came to mashing potatoes. Elliot often wondered if she thought of his dad when she was forcefully pressing them into the pan, spending her pent up aggression on vegetables. She was never the sort to have done anything aggressive or physical towards his dad in reality, but she clearly enjoyed getting her frustrations out in the kitchen.

Elliot topped up Chinook's food bowl and threw his BMX helmet down on the dining room table. He stood there frozen for a moment, staring at the back of his mum's head as she busied herself. He was debating whether or not to tell her about the men and the cave. He was hesitant. He knew that if he had told his mum that he had followed two strangers on his bike across the town's busy roads, leading him to a dangerous cave off a cliff face, his life really wouldn't be worth living. His argument was that he and Georgie should go to the police and raise the alarm. Whatever the outcome, the men would be rattled enough to leave Northshore and he could quickly go back to not worrying about them. But then he was afraid that making himself known to the police would in turn make him known to the men and this could somehow put his family, his mum and sister in jeopardy. Georgie had decided to ask her dad to speak to Simon first, hoping it would lead to some answers, maybe he should just leave it at that. Elliot's brain felt like it was in a washing machine, with so many thoughts trying to be processed at once and his emotions were getting the better of him. He wondered if he was having a panic attack as his heart rate didn't seem to want to slow down and he could now feel it beating from the sides of his head. Elliot decided to quietly make his excuses and go upstairs to avoid any awkward conversations with his mother, who always knew when he was hiding something.

Across the street Georgie was reading the note her dad had left on the kitchen table. He'd decided to pop to the cemetery to lay flowers at his parents' gravestone. It was their wedding anniversary in a few days' time and he liked to mark the occasion for them with flowers. He would also always take a miniature bottle of Moet & Chandon champagne with him. After taking a generous swig for himself, he'd toast the anniversary and pour the rest over their grave, as they always did enjoy a glass together. Georgie felt awful, they were going to visit the cemetery together and she had completely forgotten about it. She assumed her dad hadn't mentioned it as she was busy making a new friend and starting to settle into life at Northshore. Georgie knew he'd prefer her to make friends, but she still felt that she'd let him down. She knew he wouldn't be long; the cemetery was only a short drive away and he had picked the flowers up the day before. But Georgie had a lot on her mind and needed to speak to someone.

Without hesitating, she picked up the yellow phone off the Mickey Mouse receiver and dialled in Mr and Mrs Weavers phone number that she knew off by heart. The dial tone warned her that she had dialled an incorrect number and she glared at the phone in disgust. The number was right, what's wrong with this phone she thought? Then looking at their new number her dad had written on a 'post it note' next to the phone, she realised she now needed to dial the area code first. Something she hadn't needed to worry about before. She got through straight away on her second attempt and let their phone ring an extra ten times before deciding to hang up. She remembered that they play skittles at the town community hall on a Saturday afternoon with their friends and wouldn't return home until around four o'clock. She stood there alone, fighting with excitement but also a little concern. She had been seduced by the mystery of the cave and she couldn't shake it out of her mind. Georgie held her key to the garage in her hand, picking at it with her thumb nail. After what she saw there, she couldn't help run the moves through her head on how she'd scale the wall and gain access to the small hole at the top. She even wondered if she could convince her dad to go there with her in the morning, but she knew he would never agree to that. The only way she was going to get to solve the mystery of the cave, was alone. All she needed was her climbing harness, her climbing shoes and a little time.

Outside parked in their black Land Rover Defender, high up on the main road looking down into Georgie and Elliot's cul-de-sac, Dominik and Dutch sat devising their next steps. So far Dominik's plan had worked beautifully. The temptation for two nosey kids had now embroiled them in the men's business, whether they liked it or not and Dominik's plan had paid off. They now knew exactly where the children lived. Dutch and Dominik debated their next move, a car was parked outside the boy's house but there was nothing outside the girl's. It was highly likely she was alone. One option for the men was blackmail. With the girl alone in her house, they could easily force their way in and frighten her to return back to the cave with them. They could then make her climb the cave wall, with the threat of harm if she refused. The town was quiet, the men knew full well that if either of the children decided to call the police they'd be so bored in the local station that they'd be knocking on the kid's doors in less than twenty minutes. Looking down at his watch Dutch noticed ten of those had already past. Dominik's plan all along avoided using violence and threat, but he was starting to think it would be too complicated to implicate. He wanted to entice the children to the cave, so they had a taste of what was there, then in turn it would lead them back to their houses allowing the men to hold all the cards. Everything so far had gone like clockwork, the question now was could they approach the children and convince them to join in and help them with their quest, or were more forceful methods necessary?

'So, what's our next move, are we going to sit here all afternoon?' Dominik was starting to get impatient, while Dutch was still trying to process their options in his head.

'It's been twenty-five minutes, if they had decided to call the cops they would have been here by now. I say we come back when it's dark. I'm not a fan of the idea but I think we're going to need to use intimidation. These look like smart kids, I don't think the draw of a hundred quid would do it with these two.' he said.

This was now part of the job for Dutch, he knew they needed help gaining access to the caves and he saw Georgie and Elliot as their quickest and only option.

'We know where they live, they're the right size. I think a little bit of 'gentle' persuasion will get us what we need. Let's get back to the unit and get the rest of the stuff. Hopefully Madeline is back from the airport and we can fill her in.' Dutch turned the ignition of the 4x4, the turbo diesel engine wailed to life. He slipped it into first gear and took one last look down towards Georgie's house.

'I hope the girl's father will be home when we come back later, more leverage. Then we get to business.' He sounded ominous as he depressed the hand brake and accelerated away down the road.

Staring at the climbing gear in her bag, Georgie's conscience kicked in and she started to think how upset her father would be with her if she went climbing the cave without him. He always insisted that a climb was never a climb if you were on your own. It was a sure-fire way of booking yourself an appointment at the local accident and emergency. She decided to hold off and look for a quick bite to eat in the kitchen, contemplating telling her dad everything.

Madeline Wolf arrived back at the body shop not a moment too soon. She had grown tired of the constant small talk from the taxi driver and his poor taste in music. She still tipped him generously after the return trip and on exiting the car she could see Dominik waiting for her in the doorway of the unit. She sensed urgency in his body language and wondered what mess he had caused now. Her high heels clopped in a steady rhythm on the concrete as she approached him, he tossed his half-smoked Café Crème mini cigar to the ground as he straightened himself up to talk.

'There's been a development in the last few hours, we'll need to fill you in.' he said.

'I trust there isn't anything wrong at the caves Dominik?'

'No not all Madame, it looks like we have secured a volunteer to help us.' he said with an unpleasant tone, before spitting a small leaf of tobacco from his mouth.

'That was quick work, is it the friend from the Cirque de Paris you mentioned, that friend of a friend?' Madeline asked genuinely interested.

'Non-Madame let's go inside we don't have much time.'

Madeline suspected more foul play from Dominik and wasn't quite sure she was going to like what he had to say. As Madeline entered the upstairs office, Dutch was zipping up a kit bag, he seemed almost relieved to see her.

'Did you get your belongings okay at the airport?' he asked

'Yes, thank you, it's waiting for me at the hotel. Now can you please explain to me what is going on?' she snapped, avoiding any more pleasantries with the charming American.

Dutch began to fill Madeline in on the day's events. How they had tried and failed to recruit two young boys to help them at the caves, but then discovered they were being watched by two different youngsters. One of which turned out to be the girl they had encountered the day before at the petrol station. Madeline was furious that the men had led the children to the caves and she quickly ran out of insults to throw at them. The thought of someone other than her and her men being there made her feel nauseated. Pacing back and forth the dark office she accused Dominik of jeopardising the secret of the caves and insinuated that Dutch was a fool for going along with his half-baked plan. Madeline grabbed hold of a spherical Swarovski crystal paperweight from the desk and launched it against the wall. It exploded into thousands of tiny glass shards just behind Dominik's head. He knew she was aiming for him. Madeline now stood there with her fingers pinched on the bridge of her nose, with her eyes shut as she gathered her thoughts. Not expecting such a violent outburst, Dominik stood there motionless looking at Dutch awaiting whatever was coming next. As much as he had messed up, he still couldn't walk away from this job and he needed Madeline to forgive and forget once more.

Madeline dropped her arms to her sides and took a seat on the dusty old leather sofa that sat in front of the desk. Dominik didn't need to say anything, he got a fresh glass and poured her a healthy serving of her favourite schnapps. She received it without looking at him and started to drink. She downed the entire glass straight away and sat there playing with the empty tumbler in her hands. Dutch watched silently, not wanting to poke the lioness anymore, afraid of getting bitten.

'So, you know where these kids live, and you tell me the girl is alone?' she said.

'Well that was just over an hour ago Madame, her father or mother may be with her now.' Dominik replied softly and not with his usual toxic demeanour.

'Here's what we're going to do, time isn't on our side after the business with the landlord. People will be around here asking questions anytime now. That's the last of the equipment we need in that bag, everything else is there I trust?'

'Yes Ma'am.' Dutch now joined the conversation.

'Then we go now, we go to this little witch's house and we take her. If her parents are there we take them too as collateral. She'll cooperate if we apply the right kind of pressure. Are you confident she can climb Dutch?'

'I've put as many pitons in as possible and I can assist from below to a degree, but we're going to have to take the risk. Most kids can climb, especially when there's a gun pointing at them.'

'Then it's decided, we leave in ten minutes. Dutch, we'll need some cable ties and duct tape, I'll fill you both in how we go about this en route. Now leave me while I change out of these clothes.' she said.

Madeline started to remove her business clothes as Dominik and Dutch left to prepare the Land Rover. She closed the office door and locked it but not at the risk of the men seeing her change. She knew they would respect her privacy. After pulling on a pair of combat trousers, Dr Marten boots and a military field jacket, she turned to the back page of her Filofax that was sitting on the desk. There was a phone number under the heading 'Northshore Spa and Hotel', she dialled the number methodically whispering the numbers out loud as she typed. Placing the phone to her ear, it was seconds before the receptionist answered the call.

'Put me through to Room 24 please, inform them Madeline Wolf is calling…' after a moment's pause she heard a solitary 'yes' from the other end of the line.

'Be at the location in two hours and bring the walkie talkie I gave you, don't be late or our arrangement is over.'

She hung up, knowing the person at the other end of the call had understood her instruction. It was now down to her, the men and the race against the clock.

Thomas Rivers sat astounded, diligently listening to Georgie relay her and Elliot's earlier adventures. He had returned from the cemetery to find Georgie suspiciously bagging up her climbing gear in the front porch of their new house. Upon questioning Georgie, he knew something was wrong and sat her down to get the truth out of her. Georgie came clean and told him everything, the bullies being approached by the men in the Land Rover, the bike chase to the beach and the discovery of the hidden cave. Initially Thomas was furious with Georgie for following two dangerous strangers and risking her life along the cliff face to gain entrance to a mysterious cave. He had to swallow his anger and think how his wife would have dealt with the situation. He could hear her voice reminding him that Georgie was in one piece, home safe and still learning. He couldn't stop his disappointment being apparent and Georgie knew she had upset him. Sitting there now she understood why, and a wave of guilt washed over her.

'I'm sorry dad I didn't think.' she said.

'No, you didn't… Look, it's fine, you're okay so let's try and forget about it. They didn't harm you or see you by the sounds of it, so we'll let it go.'

'No, we can't let it go. We need to tell the police, what about Simon?'

'Simon? What's he got to do with it?' he said puzzled.

'I forgot to tell you, I saw his van at the body shop last night, so he must have had a conversation with them. Maybe he knows what they're up too?!'

'I don't know Georgie, I don't want to pry into his business.' Thomas said growing aggravated at Georgie's persistent attitude.

'Please just call him dad, just call him to meet up and side-line it in somehow?'

Her dad sighed, 'For goodness sake Georgie, fine. I'll call him, but then that's it, no more. You drop it. You understand me?'

Thomas marched to the telephone and pulled out Simon Jenkins' business card out from his wallet. He had given it to him the day before at the café. Georgie stared at her dad and he stared back as he stood waiting for someone to answer the phone. After a few rings Thomas was close to hanging up when finally, a lady answered the phone.

'Oh hello, is Simon there please?' he asked.

Georgie watched as her dad's face turned a pale grey right in front her, she didn't need to know what her dad was about to say it was very obvious something wasn't right.

'He didn't come home last night? No, I'm sorry, I don't. I saw him yesterday afternoon at the café and was calling to see if he'd like to meet up next week, I'm an old friend.'

Thomas stood there listening, Georgie could hear a muffled frantic sounding female voice from where she was standing and started to think the worst.

'I hope he turns up soon, please tell him I called. Bye for now.' he placed the yellow phone back onto the Mickey Mouse receiver and turned his attention back to Georgie.

'Georgie what time did you see Simon's van at that old unit last night?'

'It must have been close to five o'clock, only ten minutes or so before I got home.'

Thomas cast his mind back to the previous evening. He knew she was right, he remembered checking the time to see how long she had been out before she happened to walk through the door around five fifteen.

'Sweetheart, Simon didn't go home last night. His wife sounds like she's in a right panic. She said his colleagues saw him leave his hire shop around four, but nobody's seen him since.'

As Thomas finished talking there was a firm knock at the front door that made Georgie jump. Thomas wasn't expecting anyone and wondered who it would it be. Through the frosted glass in the front door and thanks to the security light outside, he could see it was a woman. Georgie was worried, after seeing Simon's van at the body shop then hearing he hadn't returned home last night, many scenarios started to run through her mind. As Thomas opened the front door, stood in front of him was a woman with dark red hair. He didn't recognise her, and she didn't say a word. Out of nowhere a powerful man barged in between the door frame and the woman, grabbing him by the throat and pushing him back onto the stairs, pinning him down with his knee pressed hard into Thomas' chest. Georgie started screaming and ran towards her father to help but it was no use, the woman ran at her grabbing around her arms and dragged her to the floor. Then the Frenchman appeared in the doorway, struggling to walk on his plaster cast without his crutches. He dragged his broken leg as he walked toward Georgie, opening a plastic bag of cable ties spilling some onto the floor. As he approached her, she could smell his body odour and cigar smoke on his breath. He was rough with her hands as he bound them together tight with a cable tie. The large man had thrown Georgie's dad to the ground face first and pressed his foot into Thomas' back causing him to scream out in pain. He pulled his arms together and tied him the same way Georgie had been tied by the Frenchman. The red-haired woman pulled on a roll of duct tape and sealed both Georgie and Thomas' mouths shut. They were both bound and gagged on the floor of the living room, frantically fighting to get free.

Looking at them flailing around on the floor, the Frenchman kicked Thomas hard in the side of his chest, causing him to yell behind the tape in agony. Georgie watched on as her father became motionless from the pain and she cried as she tried to get close to him. The Frenchman knelt down next to Georgie's face placing his index finger on his lips signalling for her to be quiet. What Georgie saw sent a chill down her spine, gleaming in cheap gold right in front of her eyes was something she recognised at once. The Frenchman was wearing Simon Jenkins' signet ring on his middle finger. They had done something to Simon, Georgie was now sure of it. The woman began to speak in a German accent.

'I apologise for the forced entry, but we are short on time. You are both coming with us, your daughter here has a task I need her to complete. If you comply we will spare your lives, if you choose not to… well my friend here will demonstrate.'

The woman signalled to the large American who removed a handgun out from its holster and cocked it right in front of them, before pointing it directly at Thomas' head. Georgie burst into tears and struggled to breathe through her nose with her mouth cemented by the tape.

'We will help you stand, please don't fight, or we will shoot you. Our car is outside, we're going to go on a little journey somewhere. Your daughter knows exactly where.'

The woman left the house abruptly and sat waiting in the passenger seat of the Land Rover outside. She scanned around the houses to make sure nobody was watching the events unfold in this sleepy neighbourhood. The American handed his gun to the smaller Frenchman as he helped Thomas to his feet. He groaned in pain as he was lifted, Georgie knew her father's ribs were broken, and she prayed his lung hadn't been punctured also. She watched as they started to drag him away and judged by his breathing that he was okay for now. With Georgie tied up, the men confidently led Thomas out to the car together. Georgie saw her chance, she leapt up off the floor and ran towards the phone knocking it off the receiver with her shoulder. She hesitated thinking who to call. Using her nose, she keyed in the phone number for the Weavers, remembering to use the area code as quickly as she could before the men came back into the house. She dialled the number and heard the ringing tone coming from the earpiece. She stood up kicking the phone closer to the wall, so the men wouldn't notice what she had done. She could have called the police but knew they would arrive too late and to an empty house. By calling the Weavers, Georgie knew she could rely on them to speed down and help as best as they could. She prayed they'd find Elliot and that he would help them, she just hoped they were home and had answered the call.

The huge American man returned and towered over her as he emerged in through the front door. She fell backwards and tried to push herself away from him towards the kitchen, but with her hands tied together she struggled to get anywhere fast. The monster of a man was too fast and too strong. He grabbed hold of Georgie by the belt around her waist and threw her over his shoulder, she could feel the belt digging into her hips. She fought against him, but it was useless, his arms were like a vice. Walking out of the kitchen he noticed Georgie's bag lying on the hallway floor, half open with her climbing gear inside. He picked it up and threw it toward the Frenchman who caught it with his free hand, his other hand occupied by the pistol pointing at Georgie.

'Looks like our little assistant here was planning on a climb all by herself. We'll take that with us she can use them at the caves… and don't point that thing at me, I have her under control.' Dutch said.

'Oui. Hey, her name is written inside… après midi, Georgie Rivers.' the Frenchman replied and glanced down at the phone on the floor. Frowning, he picked up the yellow phone and placed it to his ear. He heard nothing, not even a dial tone and tossed the phone back to the ground.

On the outskirts of Cheltenham Mr Weaver was firmly squeezing his hand over the mouthpiece of his phone not to allow whoever was on the opposite end hear him breathing. He glanced at his watch then slammed the phone down on the receiver rushing into the living room.

'Get your shoes on Edith and dig out Georgie and Thomas' new address from the kitchen. I'll get the road map from the study and meet you outside. Our girl's in trouble!'

Without hesitating Mrs Weaver got to her feet and retrieved the address off the fridge in the kitchen, it was being held there by a miniature frame fridge magnet holding a passport sized photo of Georgie. Exactly five minutes later, the Weavers were driving faster than they normally would out of their quiet estate. Heading for the M5 in the direction of South Wales, it would be just over an hour before they arrived at Georgie's new house and Mr Weaver knew he had no time to waste.

CHAPTER TEN
AN EMPTY HOUSE

Elliot lay on his bed with his head resting on his hands, staring up at the swirly bumps in the artex ceiling above him. Wondering to himself how the decorators created that effect. He wondered if they use a brush, or maybe they use a special tool? He was busy trying to forget about the morning at the cave and was now using anything he could get his eyes on as a distraction to prevent him from confessing to his mum. It was dark outside, he knew it would be close to teatime soon and that Georgie and her father would be coming over. He wondered if talking to his mum about chasing down strangers and discovering a hidden cave off the side of a cliff would be such a great idea? Especially before having his new friend around for dinner. If his mum found out it was her idea in the first place, she may never let them see each other again. He and Georgie hadn't really come up with a plan when they arrived back at their houses. Elliot had decided to leave it up to Georgie to inform her dad and he'd roll with the consequences afterward. It had been a few hours since they returned home, and he hadn't heard anything from her. Flicking through the latest Superman comic he'd already read twice before, he dropped it onto his bed and decided to go across the road and check in with Georgie to find out how her chat had gone with her dad.

He hoped if she had told her dad, he had been lenient with her and didn't blame him for allowing her to go on a dangerous adventure in the first place. Elliot felt responsible somehow and didn't want to jeopardise the beginnings of a great friendship. He stood up and slid his feet into his battered old Reebok trainers, they were frayed, and even had the beginnings of a hole above his right big toe. He was long overdue a new pair. Since Christmas wasn't too far away, he thought he may try his luck and guilt his father into getting him a pair of the new Reebok Pumps that all the kids kept talking about at school. They were probably way overpriced, but he knew his dad would do anything to keep him happy and since he couldn't afford to give Elliot any of his time, he'd take his gifts instead as a consolation prize.

Elliot called out to his mum as he landed at the bottom of the stairs, 'Just popping over to see Georgie a minute Mum, won't be long!' when he realised she was stood right next to him making him jump.

'You've been very quiet today, everything alright?' she said.

Elliot quickly improvised, not expecting his mum to be so close to him asking questions.

'Yeah… yeah all good. Just been listening to music and reading for a bit, we went for a long ride this morning, so my legs were worn out!'

'You're being a little weird Elliot.' she said.

'Am I? I don't mean to be.'

Tracey studied Elliot, waiting for him to say something. He stood there looking awkward, she knew there was something on his mind that he wanted to tell her. For some reason he didn't feel comfortable and she could tell, she could read her son like a book. She decided to let it go, he'd tell her in his own time.

'Go on then, off you pop.' she said simply, and Elliot gave half a smile as he headed out waiting for Chinook to follow him before he shut the door.

Under the amber glow of the street lights, Elliot was surprised at how quickly it had gotten dark. He had let a good few hours slip him by worrying away in his bedroom. Thomas Rivers' car was parked on the driveway and he again wondered if he might be in trouble, that was if Georgie had decided to say anything at all he thought.

Chinook as usual had run ahead of Elliot and had started barking and growling by the front door. Once Elliot had caught up he could see why. The front door was wide open, and the telephone was smashed over the hallway. He stepped inside the newly decorated house and called out for Georgie, there was no answer. Walking into the living room, he noticed a drop of what looked like fresh blood on the cream carpet and there were two cable ties lying on the ground. Chinook frantically ran around the downstairs sniffing at the floor, stopping occasionally to bark at Elliot before carrying on. Elliot froze, he didn't know what to do. He was about to run home when an old man appeared in the hallway.

'Hello young man, I'm looking for Georgie and Thomas Rivers, I believe this is their house?' the man was worryingly looking around and he called out Georgie and Thomas' names.

Confused and scared Elliot ran past him, nearly knocking over an old lady as he ran down the driveway. He could see their car, a Rover 214 still ticking over with the driver's door wide open. Elliot ran as fast as he could back to his house, not knowing what to do or who to trust. His friend and possibly her father had gone missing and two new strangers were looking for her. Chinook stayed outside, barking in the confusion as Elliot slammed the back door shut looking petrified. Tracey immediately ran to her son after hearing the slam of the door, she found Elliot sitting on the floor with his back pressing against the door. As she approached him, he looked up to her with tears forming in his eyes.

'Please don't be mad Mum, I think Georgie is in trouble!'

Elliot stood up and Tracey pulled her sobbing son into her arms. With no time to process what was happening the front door bell rang repeatedly, until she opened the door.

'I'm so sorry to trouble you Miss, we've just driven a very long way and we need some help. It's about Georgie and Thomas Rivers. They recently moved in opposite, it's quite urgent, we're friends of theirs.'

An elderly couple were stood on the doorstep both looking distressed. Tracey didn't understand why they were there, or why they were so desperate to talk about Georgie, but she knew it concerned Elliot somehow. Tracey guarded Elliot and Chinook circled the old man sniffing at his legs, the man showed no fear or attention towards the intimidating dog, it was as though Chinook wasn't even there.

'Edith, do you still have that photo in your purse?' the elderly man held his hand out toward the lady. She reached into her bag and from her purse she pulled out a small polaroid photograph of them and Georgie, enjoying an ice cream in a well-kept back garden. He stretched his arm out toward Tracey and Elliot, allowing them to take in the photo.

'This is us with Georgie in the summer, we're Mr and Mrs Weaver. I don't know if she's mentioned us to you, but we're close friends of hers and Thomas. I received a phone call from her, we believe she's been kidnapped. I get the feeling your young lad there may know something?'

The word 'kidnapped' hit Tracey like a punch in the chest and she dropped slightly to Elliot's eye level holding his arms tight, slightly shaking him as she spoke.

'What's going on Elliot, where did you go with Georgie today?!' she demanded, she knew he'd been hiding something all along. Seeing the concern on the woman's face, Mr Weaver calmly interjected.

'Miss, my name is Sidney, and this is my wife Edith. Can we please sit down and talk with you and your son for a moment, I don't think we have much time to waste.'

Tracey stood up and tilted her head signalling for the Weavers to enter the house. Chinook calmly bounded in ahead of them and lay down flat on his belly with his chin resting on his paws, his ears stood high to attention.

Elliot walked into the living room and sat down, he knew he had to tell his mum and Georgie's friends everything. Staring at the floral patterns in the carpet, not able to look them in the eye feeling embarrassed. Elliot started with how he and Georgie decided to follow two suspicious men and how it had led them to the beach. The more Elliot talked the less ashamed he became, and he was giving them every detail from the type of car they followed, to the description of the men and how Georgie discovered the entry into the cave through the waterfall. Mr Weaver listened intently, taking everything in whilst Tracey could barely talk at the shock of what her son had been up to. All she could think of was that it was a blessing he was home safe and how worried she was for Georgie and her dad.

It only took a few minutes for Elliot to fill his mum and Mr Weaver in on the earlier events with Georgie and he knew Mr Weaver was right, there was no time to waste. He had to get to Georgie and help her, and he had to get there fast. Mr Weaver stayed calm and was thankful for Elliot's honesty, he looked down at the ground as though he was wondering what to say next. He stood up and told Tracey they would go over to the Rivers' house and call the police, he then looked at Elliot.

'Elliot after I've called the police, would you take me to this cave of yours? I know they've taken Georgie there, I heard them over the phone.'

Elliot shook his head looking scared, he shouted 'No, no way it's too dangerous!' and he ran into the kitchen making it look like he was too frightened and upset to go back there. Tracey placed a hand on Mr Weaver's shoulder and asked him to give Elliot a few minutes to calm down and that she'd speak to him. Mr Weaver found it a little odd that Elliot reacted that way after speaking so calmly minutes before and wondered if the boy was up to something. He played along keeping his distance and didn't give away his suspicion before returning to Georgie's house.

Georgie and her father had been held captive in the back of the Land Rover for what felt like over an hour, maybe two? Her nose was slightly blocked from where she'd been crying, and she was finding it hard to breathe through with the duct tape firmly secured over her mouth. She knew they were back at the coast, the large American man had even stopped the car at the car park to remove the beams from the fence, she heard them clang on the ground as he easily threw them down. That must have been at least an hour ago she thought. There was no room for her and her father to move, they were bunched up in the back of the Land Rover, piled on top of each other, her arms were starting to go numb. She had been trying to squeeze her hands out from the cable ties but to no avail, she had only managed to make her wrists sore in the process. Her father's breathing was also strained, and she knew his injury needed medical attention, she blamed herself for getting them into this mess and she realised the men had been playing a game with them all along, they must have known they were being followed. She lay there trying to conserve her energy in case of a momentary lack of concentration from her captors, to allow her to escape. She stared out at the stars above, how she wished she was at home with her mum and dad cosied up on the sofa together. But things had changed, life had drastically changed and however the night panned out for Georgie and her father she knew life would never quite be the same again.

Georgie started to wonder who the woman with the German accent was. She had briefly caught a glimpse of her at the petrol station, the glamorous looking red-haired woman who had scolded the Frenchman after his altercation with Georgie. She'd given Georgie a sample of her cold gaze then, as the Land Rover had driven out of the station, making Georgie fully aware of how intimidating she could be. She hadn't said much back at the house, she hadn't needed to as the men had been so precise and swift at overpowering Georgie and her father. Few words were required, and it was clear, this woman was secretly pulling the strings. Georgie closed her eyes and hoped Elliot was okay, hoping they had left him alone. After all, if they followed them back from the cave to the estate they would know where each of them lived. She wondered if Elliot had seen what had happened and if he had called the police. Or if the Weavers had heard any of the commotion over the phone, she knew they wouldn't let her down. But she had no idea if they were home when she called, she didn't get the chance to listen on her end to whether the phone had been answered or not. Knowing her luck, the Weavers were still playing skittles with their friends.

Georgie had no more time to consider what was happening, the back door of the Land Rover swung open and the two men pulled her and her father out onto the grass. Georgie felt her arms tingle as the blood started to circulate back around and she felt the sensation of pins and needles in her fingertips. The men forced her and Thomas onto their knees, the ground felt cold and wet as the rain water started to soak into her jeans. Facing her abductors, she noticed the woman standing behind them. Georgie couldn't stand the sight of her and wanted to put all her energy into charging straight at her, but she knew her actions would be hopeless, the men were too strong.

'Georgie and Thomas Rivers.' the red-haired lady said while pulling out Thomas' bank cards from his wallet, dropping them to the ground one by one before throwing his wallet away over the cliff, down towards the sea and rocks below.

'Thomas, your daughter here likes to get involved in other people's business. My business in fact. A hundred or so yards off the edge of this cliff lies a hidden cave, undisturbed for over two hundred years. We know about it as we have spent months locating it. But your nosey little brat here found it much faster, but only as we allowed her to. My men realised Georgie and her little friend were spying on them earlier today. As it happens we need a little help in the cave. Your daughter may not only be just the right size for the job, but judging from her belongings here, may have just the right skill set.'

Madeline dropped Georgie's bag with her climbing shoes and harness right in front of her. She stood there silently glaring at them both, Thomas looked down at the bag then turned his attention back to the woman.

'Inside the cave lies a door that we can't open from the outside, for many reasons that I won't bore you with. Let's just say the man who built it made sure it wasn't easily accessible. We've come to the conclusion that we need someone of Georgie's stature to access it from behind. We've discovered a small access hole above the door, but it's too high and narrow for us to reach. We've prepped the wall ready for someone to climb it as best as we can, but there will need to be a little skill and improvisation no doubt.'

Madeline walked closer to Georgie, invading her space making her feel uncomfortable.

'You're going to climb this wall for us Georgie and fully cooperate, as Dominik here will have this gun pointed at your father the entire time. If you don't help us, we will shoot him. Then in the dead of night, we'll return to your estate and gun down that boy and his family while they sleep! Yes, we know where he lives too, am I making myself clear Georgie?!'

Georgie was furious, her heart was racing, and her adrenaline was in overdrive, her chest hurt from her heart pounding so hard. As she tried to control her temper she could feel tears of rage building up in her eyes and she screamed 'No!' as loudly as she could, but it was muffled by the duct tape covering her mouth. This world had already taken her mother from her, she wasn't about to let this woman take her friend.

'You'd better compose yourself Georgie. My name is Madeline Wolf, but you can call me Ms Wolf. We've got a long night ahead of us.' The woman's tone was precise and cold, she leaned forward and ripped off the duct tape from Georgie's mouth. Georgie yelped a little as the sting of the strong glue of the tape tore away from her skin. She opened her mouth and took in a huge breath of fresh air, it felt like she was waking up for the first time and her body thanked her for the oxygen.

'Please take that tape off my father's mouth, we can barely breath, he'll stay quiet won't you Dad?'

Thomas nodded in agreement and Madeline removed his tape quickly, making him wince in pain. Seeing her father able to breath more easily was a relief for Georgie. She took in a few more deep breaths and looked up at Madeline Wolf.

'I'll do whatever you want, just please don't hurt my dad anymore and stay away from my friend. This is my fault not his. I'll need a bit of help, but I'll get you in through that door. Just promise me you'll let us go.' she said.

Madeline studied Georgie briefly before walking over to the Land Rover and pushing the back door shut.

'You have my word. Dutch, pick them up, let's get this started.' she said.

Elliot's little act of being scared had worked to his advantage, Mr Weaver had gone across the road to Georgie's house and his mum was busy tending to his sister Alice, giving him some space to calm down. Elliot knew his mum had stored his motocross gear in the cupboard under the stairs, which he could sneak into from the kitchen. He had run into the kitchen rather than upstairs to his room on purpose, he had already built an idea of what he was going to do while he relayed his story to his mum and Mr Weaver. He knew where Georgie was, and he needed to get there quickly, he was going to save her whatever the cost. He quietly made his way into the dining room and delicately opened the cupboard under the stairs, trying not to be heard. It housed everyone's coats, shoes, umbrellas and anything else his mum had decided to shove in there. He hadn't used his motocross gear in so long, that it was buried under a pile of old clothes that had been destined for the charity shop since they moved in. He could see the top of his boots sticking up through the clothes and he climbed into the cupboard to retrieve them. It was all there, his boots, jersey and racing trousers, they were creased and a little out of shape but that didn't matter.

Trying not to drop them, he tiptoed out towards the back door. Chinook was still lying down on the living room floor and Elliot knew he'd hear the back door open. He carefully opened the kitchen window as wide as it would go, climbed up onto the work surface and dropped down into the back garden. He would have liked to have Chinook at his side, but what Elliot was planning would be too risky to have him accidentally get in the way. The garage was still unlocked from where Elliot put his BMX away earlier, he walked in and chose not to put the light on in case his mum noticed from the house. After getting changed into his racing gear he dug out his Thor Mach 5 chest protector and motocross helmet and put them on.

Elliot stood in front of his Kawasaki KX 80, the last time he rode it he struggled to control its speed. But Georgie needed him, and he needed her, he wasn't going to sit by while his friend was in trouble. It was dark out and his KX didn't come with street legal lights being an off-road motorcycle. Using some insulation tape, he wrapped two torches that he dug out from an old box to his front and rear mudguards. They weren't the brightest, but there was only so far he could go via the back lanes. He'd have to go on the road at some points and he needed to be seen, not just for his safety but everyone else on the road too. With the torches on and his helmet firmly secured, Elliot opened the garage door as wide as it would go and snuck down to the end of the drive opening the gates ready. Inside the house his mum Tracey thought it was time to speak to Elliot and as she entered the kitchen she knew instinctively that he wasn't there. She called out 'Elliot?' but there was no answer, she hurried to the bottom of the stairs and called out again up towards Elliot's room, 'Elliot?!'. Suddenly from outside she heard the sound of a motorbike being kick started to life and revving loud. By the time she realised what Elliot was doing and had opened the front door, she saw a lime green blur whiz past her as Elliot blasted out of the driveway.

'Sorry mum.' he said to himself 'But Georgie needs me.'

Across the road Mrs Weaver was stood outside getting some fresh air, she was startled at the noise of the two-stroke, single-cylinder engine as it erupted past her up and out onto the main road with Tracey running behind it, calling out Elliot's name hysterically. She stopped chasing as soon as she realised she'd never catch him. Mr Weaver still had the front door wide open while he was on the phone trying to get hold of the coast guard, he heard the commotion and ran out to the front of the house to see what was going on. As he arrived at the front of the house, he could faintly hear the sound of the motorbike fade away in the distance. Tracey was stood sobbing in the middle of the road with Chinook stood by her side, Mr Weaver ran over to comfort her.

'He's going to the cave they found, he's going to try and help them. I know he is!' Tracey shouted as she cried into Mr Weaver's shoulder.

Mr Weaver looked down at Chinook then back to his car, he hadn't wanted to go to the cave that Elliot had talked about, preferring to get the authorities to head there first. But with two children now in potential danger, he couldn't stand by and watch.

'Tracey, do you mind if I borrow Chinook? I worked with German Shepherds in the war and I'm pretty confident I can get him to lead me to Elliot. I just may need to borrow a push bike if you have one, these old legs won't be able to run alongside him I'm afraid.'

'Yes, do what you can, please don't let him get hurt. There's a bike in there.' Tracey pointed to the open door of her garage and Mr Weaver quickly grabbed the ladies Raleigh Silhouette push bike and wheeled it to the front of the house.

'Edith, you stay here and wait for the police. Tell them everything we know and that two children are at risk. Tracey, write your phone number down on this for me.' Mr Weaver handed Tracey an old business card from inside his jacket pocket and presented her with a pen from his jacket.

After she wrote her phone number down, Mr Weaver stuffed the business card and pen back into his inside jacket pocket and stepped onto the push bike. He knelt over tucking the bottom of his trouser legs into his socks.

'Right, stay by the phone and when I can I'll find the nearest payphone and call you with any news. Chinook old boy, heel!'

With his military authoritative tone, Chinook went and sat right next to Mr Weaver. He stroked his chest twice and scratched him on his back. Tracey was amazed at how submissive Chinook was to this strange man, Elliot was the only person who really had a similar control over Chinook.

'Chinook my boy, fetch Elliot' Chinook looked apprehensively at Mr Weaver, almost looking for approval.

'Don't stare at me you old dingbat, fetch Elliot!'

With his second command Chinook barked with excitement and launched into a run, Mr Weaver put his full effort into setting off on the borrowed push bike, pedalling as best he could after the dog.

Elliot's hands gripped tightly to the handlebars of the KX. He had managed so far to avoid using any main roads, keeping to the back lanes and only occasionally crossing roads to get from one lane to the other. He also managed to keep the speed sensible on the Kawasaki and hadn't had the fear of losing control that he felt when he last rode it in the company of his father. However, Elliot was quickly running out of back alleys and lanes to use. He knew he'd have to break the law and take his unlicensed motorbike onto the public highway to access the beach. It was about a mile that he'd have to cover, he prayed that the roads would be quiet and wasn't quite sure how he'd manage riding his bike with other vehicles around him. He'd only ever ridden in empty fields or on motocross tracks with other bikers up until now. This was dangerous and also a little a stupid he admitted to himself, what was he going to do if he needed to indicate at a junction or stop suddenly? His bike wasn't equipped with indicators or a brake light, it was purely for using off road.

The light's he'd taped to his mud guards were holding well, but they were by no means road legal or very bright. He decided he wasn't going to worry, Georgie was worth the risk. He inched his head out of the junction feeding from a narrow alley, the volume of the bike's engine was starting to attract attention from people using the pavements near him. He could smell the Chip Shop and the Chinese takeaway a few doors down and it made him feel nauseous. He was hungry, but the guilt of not checking on Georgie sooner and the pressure of being out on his motorbike illegally was making his stomach turn. He glanced to his left then back to his right, there was no traffic, time to move. He squeezed in the clutch with his left hand and knocked the KX into first gear with his foot. Pulling nervously quick on the throttle, he lunged forward and stalled. Being so anxious he had released the clutch out far too fast. Panicking, he pulled the kick back out and fired the bike back to life. Without checking he released the clutch once more and pulled out into the road, unwittingly straight into the path of a white Ford Fiesta that he hadn't seen coming. The car's horn screamed as the driver just caught a glimpse of Elliot as he swung out in front of him, swerving and missing Elliot's bike by inches before coming to a stop. Elliot's heart was in his mouth and the shock almost made him vomit into his helmet, but he managed to shake it off and stay calm. He felt awful and hoped whoever was driving the car didn't recognise him and weren't too shaken up.

The tarmac felt smooth under the bikes tyres and as he notched up the gears through third and into forth, he started to feel the power of the bike underneath him as he glided down towards the coast. It took him less time than he'd anticipated to reach the road that led directly to the beach and he was relieved that apart from his near miss with the Fiesta, the roads were relatively quiet. He blasted the bike down the entry road before skidding into the car park. Standing on the foot pegs of the motorbike he drove around the perimeter looking for a break in the fence so he could get through. He knew he'd struggle to remove the beams as the huge American had done so easily earlier in the day by himself. There was nothing, the fence surrounded the entire car park, he suspected the council knew people would try and take 'off road' bikes up there if they had the chance.

Elliot slowed and came to a stop, he needed to think. There had to be a way he could get up to the cliffs with the bike. He thought maybe there was access from the beach somehow, but he'd walked the full length of the beach many times with Chinook and couldn't think of any way up from there. The sea would eventually cut him off, crashing right up to the rocks and cliff face. He scanned the perimeter of the fence once more when his eyes fixed on a possibility. Laying on the ground in the corner of the car park, someone had left some scaffolding poles and beams behind from when the stonewall of the car park was being repaired. He had an idea, it was risky, but it might just work he thought. He stood his bike up using the foot stand, leaving it running and pulled the wooden beams close to the fence. They were heavy, and he struggled to get them up off the ground. He dragged one end close to the fence and stopped to get his breath back. Using all his strength, Elliot lifted one end of the beam up to rest on the top of the fence. He'd only completed a few ramp jumps before and looking at the height of the fence, this was definitely going to be his highest and the most difficult. He just hoped the wood wasn't rotten, he walked halfway up the beam and hopped up and down to test it. It felt firm under foot, but whether it would hold the weight of both him and the bike he wasn't so sure. He was also concerned by how narrow it was, a slight misjudgement and he'd crash face first into the beams of the fence. Once more Elliot swallowed his fears and aimed his Kawasaki directly at the makeshift ramp ahead of him. He knew he'd need a lot of speed and careful precision to get over the fence successfully. He twisted back the accelerator making his back-wheel spin in the loose dirt, causing the bike to burst forwards toward the ramp. He leaned forward pressing all his weight to the front of the bike, making sure his front wheel stayed on the ground. He managed to get the bike into third gear a few meters before the bike touched the ramp. The beam slid forward against the fence when the front tyre made contact, but when the back wheel came onto the ramp its weight held it firm. Pulling the throttle all the way back, the bike bellowed up the ramp and Elliot flew into the field opposite, landing almost perfectly with the back wheel touching the ground shortly before the front. Elliot brought the bike to a swift stop and looked back as the ramp bounced around before falling back to the car park floor. He let out a huge sigh of relief and laughed out loud. Then turning his attention back to the job in hand, he looked up towards the cliffs and was swiftly reminded of his mission.

CHAPTER ELEVEN
THE CLIMB

The cold rock floor of the cave was painfully uncomfortable underneath Thomas Rivers. His hands were both cable-tied behind his back and he was sitting with a Beretta M9 semi-automatic pistol pointing at his right temple. His rib cage was sore, his breathing was becoming more difficult and he knew he had at least one broken rib that would put him out of action for easily a week. Not the best start at a new job he thought, not that he cared at that moment. He was amazed that these people had discovered this mystifying cave. He watched on helplessly as Madeline Wolf paced impatiently around it. She was redirecting spotlights and checking her watch as his daughter prepared herself to climb what looked to him to be a very dangerous wall. Thankfully, they agreed to Georgie's request and removed the duct tape from his mouth. As much as it hurt him to breathe, getting air in was a lot easier now. Feeling helpless, he struggled internally with the temptation to shout at their three captors. He was angry and frightened for Georgie, he wanted his daughter with him, not scaling dangerous heights and being forced to do dangerous deeds for crooks. She was only twelve years old for goodness sake. But with a barrel of a gun aimed directly at him, he knew he was better off preserving his energy and keeping quiet for his sake and most importantly Georgie's. Thomas sat there going through each of their names in his head, Madeline, Dutch and Dominik. He wondered if Madeline was using the men's given names, whether she would be that nonchalant or if they had used pseudonyms for the purpose of their job. The name's matched the faces he thought, and he sat there scrutinising them. He'd never overpower the American; he was too strong, but Dominik and Madeline… if the moment presented itself and he could get Georgie to safety, he'd have no qualms with causing them injury if necessary to escape. Thomas loathed violence, it was against his beliefs and principles as a doctor, his ambition in life was to help people not to hurt them and he felt conflicted. But in this threatening situation, he had to defend himself and his daughter, any way he could.

Georgie ran her hand along the cool rock wall, feeling every bump under her fingertips. The rock was coarse in places but smooth overall. She knew she'd have no problem climbing it, she'd climbed worse before. She made a mental note of places where she could get a firm footing and planned her approach silently to herself. Dutch was busy next to her, getting the ropes and pulleys in order to assist her as she climbed. She held her harness loose in her hand, contemplating her chances of escape. But seeing her father uncomfortable on the floor with a gun pointed at his head reminded her that this wasn't an option, not just yet anyway. She dropped the harness to the floor and stepped into the leg loops before pulling it up to position and tightened the buckle. Usually her dad would double check to make sure everything was tight and correct, but that wouldn't happen today. It was solely her responsibility to keep herself safe and in doing so keeping her father safe too. Madeline marched over to Georgie, she already despised the woman and could tell by the unimpressed look on her face that she was about to complain about something. It was obvious to Georgie that Madeline was from a privileged background. She stank of superiority, it was clear that she had never had to work particularly hard for anything in life and she had been nurtured by the upper classes. She wondered why she seemed to be putting so much of her time and energy into discovering what was concealed behind this old door in the cave. If a woman of wealth was desperate to obtain it, then it must be something priceless, or maybe even powerful? Georgie admitted to herself that she was curious too.

'What's taking so long? Why isn't she half way up this damn wall already?' Madeline barked.

'Won't be long now, she's got her harness and shoes on. As soon as I attach her to this carabiner she's all set.' Dutch replied, while still arranging and tightening the ropes he had installed ready for Georgie's climb.

He grabbed hold of Georgie's harness and pulled her towards him and clasped the carabiner to her belay loop, he then connected a spare rope to her haul loop on the back of her harness, which took Georgie by surprise.

'You may need to use this as a top rope once you're through the hole. We have no idea what you're gonna find when you're through. Try and anchor it to something before you go in, you may need it as a lifeline to pull yourself back out or lower yourself down.'

Georgie looked into Dutch's eyes and could tell he was uncomfortable with making her climb, whether it because of her age or because he didn't trust her. He turned away and pulled down on the slack end of the rope, tightening it up on her end. She felt her harness grip against her legs, she was suddenly reminded of her biking injury and flinched as the harness sent a wave of pain up through her body. Thankfully it was short lived and after a quick adjustment, she was more comfortable.

'Ready to go here Madeline. Georgie get into position over here and use these pitons to start.' Dutch's voice was loud and filled the cave. All eyes were on Georgie as she apprehensively took position at the foot of the cave wall, ready to start her climb to the opening.

'Don't mess this up girl, or Daddy here stops breathing.' Madeline hissed at Georgie. She then turned on the two video cameras that were set up on tripods, one pointing at the old door and the other at Georgie.

Georgie turned to look at her father once more before taking a deep breath and began her climb using the anchor pitons that Dutch had installed. She navigated up them with ease and ran out of the pegs to hold onto in no time. Reaching the last anchor and only being just under a third of the way up the wall, Georgie stopped and looked down. Madeline was watching intently, and Dutch was monitoring her, keeping a firm hold of the rope.

'I'm out of pitons, you're going to have to slack off the rope so I can go freestyle.' Georgie shouted down, Dutch understood and hand over hand started to loosen his bind with Georgie.

She felt the rope on the front of her harness go slack and she pulled it out further to free herself. She knew if she fell she'd hit this point of the wall and Dutch would have her secure by the rope, although her pelvis and spine wouldn't thank her for it. Dipping her hand into her chalk bag she dusted her hands and readied herself to climb free of the anchors. Stretching as high as she comfortably could, she got a firm grip on the rock and heaved herself up supporting herself by using her feet on the pitons. Examining the rock, she could see there were plenty of cracks and natural grips she could use. Below, Madeline held her breath as the young girl began to ascend higher and higher looking like a human spider crawling along the cave wall. Georgie soon started to feel the cave start close in around her, as she climbed further up the wall. She could feel the huge rock formation behind her narrowing, giving her limited space to move. She knew that an adult wouldn't have made it as high as she had. The natural formation of the rock made a very narrow opening to get through, but her goal was constantly in sight.

Georgie couldn't always go up, she had to navigate herself horizontally making the best use of the wall in front of her. Her fingers and toes were starting to ache, it had been a few weeks since her last climb and she was feeling out of practice. She was able to rest her hands at times by pressing her back firmly up against the rock behind her and using her feet as an anchor on the wall. Madeline found it uncomfortable viewing when Georgie did this, she thought the girl was being careless and risky.

The gap between the cave walls was getting narrower the closer she got to her destination and the stalactites were also beginning to get dangerously close, hanging long from the cave ceiling. Georgie decided to take a rest and attempted to install a wall nut that would hopefully stop her falling if she was to lose her grip. She noticed a perfect crack in the rock to fit it and then thread her safety rope through, she hoped she wouldn't need it, but she was now meters away from the opening. After securing the nut and taking a moment to rest, Georgie looked up to analyse what lay ahead of her. She could see now that the stalactites would start to present a serious problem if she wasn't careful and she wanted to avoid clashing with them or pressing into one of their sharp points.

Thomas Rivers felt physically sick. His injuries aside, he felt nervous and frightened for Georgie. All he could see was the rope occasionally swaying at the base of the wall, he was completely powerless to do anything other than watch. Madeline and Dutch still had their attentions directed upwards, which was a mild comfort for him that she was still going. Dutch glanced at Madeline, she hadn't taken her eyes off Georgie as she began her climb and he could see the greed growing in her eyes. Looking up at the young girl, he was impressed with her resilience and how quickly she had scaled the wall. But he knew her biggest challenge was ahead of her, as the space started to close in.

'What are you waiting for girl get going?!' Madeline called up, getting tired of waiting for Georgie to resume her climb.

Georgie ignored her, she just needed an extra few seconds to compose herself before moving on. It wasn't like Madeline could do anything to her where she was, Georgie in some ways held some cards of her own now.

'I've got a cramp in my calf, it's easing off. Just give me a minute.' Georgie replied.

Dutch held onto the rope almost embarrassed by Madeline and her behaviour toward Georgie, he wanted to tell her to shut up, but didn't want to risk losing out on his cut of the deal.

Georgie started climbing again, her rope was occasionally getting caught up in the nut she had installed in the wall, having to twist herself around the long stalactites wasn't helping and the space started to become more and more confined. Georgie could feel a slight breeze of fresh air and noticed a small hole just above her head. As she got close, she could hear subtle movement. Slowly placing her hand on the outside of the hole for extra stability, she pulled herself up to peer inside. Staring back at her was an angry seagull mother, protecting its young in her nest. Georgie held her breath and backed away from the hole, she felt a cold sweat run down her back and fought against the urge to panic. Of all the things to have a phobia about and all the places for them to show up, it had to be now. She swallowed her fear knowing the last time she let a seagull get the better of her it landed her in hot water with Dominik. She had to stay calm and knew she had to get past the nest to get to her destination. She looked around, there was no way to avoid passing the nest. There were sharp stalactites hanging down on both sides of her, not allowing much manoeuvrability. Taking in slow breaths she started to move past the hole, pulling herself up as steadily as she could as not to disturb the gull. Her face got past unscathed, but the bird started squawking angrily and she could hear the chicks squeaking with fright. As she slowly lifted the rest of her body past, the mother gull started to stab at her torso repeatedly with its beak and nipping at her clothes aggressively. Georgie panicked and batted at the bird with her hand losing her grip. She slid down at a fast rate, grazing her face and knees on the cave walls as she tried to stop herself, clawing onto anything she could. Madeline and Dutch watched from below, swiftly moving out of the way of falling debris. Dutch pulled down on the rope in case Georgie's nut didn't hold before looking up and realising Georgie had come to a sudden stop. She let out a loud cry of pain, Thomas jumped to his feet only to be pushed back down by Dominik using the gun as a prod.

'You stay put!' he shouted as he pressed the pistol against Thomas' forehead, Thomas reluctantly knelt back down, desperate to check on his daughter.

Dutch looked up and could see Georgie suspended by her safety harness and the rope as she slowly tried to adjust herself back into a climbing position.

'Georgie! What's going on?!' he bellowed, Madeline looked agitated and annoyed that the girl had messed up.

'I'm okay, there's a seagull nest up here and I got attacked by an angry mother. I'm a bit sore, but I'm okay.' Georgie regained her composure and shook off the fright of the fall.

'Georgie, you're doing great. Chalk your hands now and stuff your chalk bag between you and the bird. You shouldn't really need it once you're past the nest!' Dutch yelled.

Georgie regained a grip on the wall and was annoyed that she hadn't thought to do that herself.

'Good idea! I'll give it a try.' she replied.

Madeline was starting to get irritated by Georgie and Dutch, she wondered if he was becoming fond of the girl and interjected.

'Girl, in all seriousness if you don't get it together I'm going to cut this rope so you work harder. Now get on with it!' she screamed, glaring at Dutch.

He knew she was putting him in his place and he returned his concentration back to Georgie not engaging a response.

Georgie felt a wave of panic come over her. This woman was desperate and irrational, and she had a gun pointed at her father below, she started to imagine the worst. She removed her chalk bag and held it between her teeth and started her ascent once more, moving quicker this time. As she neared the angry gull, she stayed low out of harm's way and pushed the chalk bag up and into the hole. It didn't fill the hole entirely, but it may just give her valuable seconds to get past unharmed. Pulling herself up slowly, Dutch's idea worked. She felt the gull bashing up against the bag, but its beak didn't jab into her this time. She reached up with her left hand and finally, she felt what she was after. The texture of the rock had changed and now she was feeling the soft mortar left by Klaus Wolfgang and his men over two hundred years ago. Arriving level with the entrance was easy and she now had an opening that allowed her a good surface to grip. Pulling herself up and pressing with her legs against the stalactites and the ceiling behind her, she pushed her head and chest up into the opening. She lay there for a moment feeling relieved that she alone had managed such a difficult climb and under immense pressure. Through the hole she could hear more water, a river must flow through the cave? She wondered if it was the same river that fed the waterfall at the entrance? Remembering Dutch's instruction, she removed the spare rope from her harness and tied one end around her waist then inserted another nut just above the opening into a firm crack in the rock. She tied the other end securely and yanked as hard as she could, it felt secure. She released the rope that was being held by Dutch and he felt it go slack down on the ground. He looked at Madeline then looked up at Georgie.

'She's made it.' he said.

Madeline punched the air excitedly and checked her watch, time was ticking for them and she needed the girl to be faster. Madeline wanted to be out of Northshore that night, the sooner the better.

High up and all alone, Georgie started to crawl head first through a small tunnel that was no longer than three meters. She had never felt claustrophobic before, but this made her dizzy, the walls seemed to be getting narrower the further in she went. It was dark where she was heading, she didn't have powerful spotlights to light it up like the cave below her. But thankfully, Dutch had slipped a small Duracell Durabeam torch into her pocket. She managed to pull it out, despite having limited room to move her arms and flipped it open with her chin to ignite the torch. Placing it in her teeth she shuffled through the entrance using her elbows. She noticed it was laced with man-made loose mortar and damp soil. The years had taken its toll and Georgie felt the mortar crumbling as she crawled through, desperately trying to stay calm. She worried that the small tunnel would cave in all around her as the mortar seemed to dent and move, crumbling onto her as she delicately inched through. She could feel the filth rubbing into her clothes and the air started to feel damp as she gently neared the other side. As her head breached the exit, she stopped to ensure there wasn't a sheer drop there to welcome her. Pointing the torch ahead of her, she found a frayed old rope secured to the old mortar below the exit. Georgie found some comfort that someone had been there previously, and she hoped the rope would still able to bear her weight.

'They were right.' she said out loud. She stretched her hand down to touch the rope, but in doing so she felt herself start to slide forward. The tunnel exit was collapsing as the mortar gave way, crumbling underneath and around her. Georgie reached for the old rope, as she wrapped her left hand around it she felt it pull away from the wall, only holding her there for a brief second before it became loose in her hand. She started to fall fast, face first out of the tunnel with mortar and loose rock falling all around her. She was thrown around like a rag doll, bashing against the walls and screaming as she fell. Every hit and crack sent pulses of pain through her body. She had no idea how far she'd fall until the top rope would tighten and save her, she heard the clatter of the torch hit the ground then suddenly she felt the piercing sharp snap of the rope as it stiffened up, breaking her fall once again. Her back felt like it had been sliced in two as she hung there suspended upside down. Staring at the cave floor that was no more than a foot beneath her face, Georgie gently swayed as the dim light from the small torch was shining up at her. She started to sob, not from the pain, but the realisation of the situation she had gotten herself into. Her father suffering outside, not only physically but also psychologically and knowing full well he would be despising seeing his daughter and only family member risking her life.

She had to be strong and get through this, it was up to her to get them out of this mess. After wiping away her tears she opened her eyes and reached down to pick up the torch. The casing had become loose and she managed to squeeze it back together before pointing it around her. The old wooden door was now right in front of her and to the left-hand side of it, she could see ropes secured to the wall. Aiming the torch at the ropes she could see that an old pulley system had been installed, amazingly it looked to Georgie as though it could have once belonged to part of an old ship.

CHAPTER TWELVE
OPENING THE DOOR

Georgie straightened herself out and pulled herself up on her rope. Untying the rope to release herself was quite the task, as the knot had overtightened from the fall. After a few minutes she managed to free herself and drop to the floor, adding to her already long list of bruises. Her legs were shaking, and her body ached from the beating that the cave had already served her. Now she was back on her own two feet, she took the time to look around the area she had fallen into. It appeared as though the door was merely blocking the entrance to a larger set of caves. She wanted to investigate, but her part of the deal was over. All she had to do was open the door and Madeline would supposedly honour her side of the bargain and let them both go free. She stood there considering her options and ran the scenarios through her head. In reality Madeline wouldn't let them go, it would be too untidy, too many loose ends.

If she already had something done to Simon, then no doubt they would do the same to her and her dad. She needed an extra bargaining chip to secure her safety and staring at the age-old door she got her answer. Georgie noticed whoever built it had recessed it into the ground slightly, probably to stop people from forcing it open from the outside, 'Very clever,' she said to herself. The rope was so old on the door that she wasn't confident that the pulley system would work, especially as the rope was covered in a filthy sort of mould. Georgie gripped the rope and slowly pulled down with all her strength. The ropes tightened around the wheels of the pulleys, squeaking as they began to turn. The door started to break free from its hold, releasing a plume of dust as it raised. Madeline and Dutch took a step back from the opposite side of the door as it opened. Neither of them taking their eyes off the spectacle in front of them and quietly amazed that the girl had made it. Georgie was surprised at just how easy it was to lift the huge door, it was now just below waist height and she knew this was her only opportunity to get an advantage. She held the door in place and called out.

'That's it, it won't go any higher! It's stuck.' she yelled.

Madeline crouched down and rolled underneath the half open door desperate to see what was behind it. Without hesitating, Dutch knelt down and started to move under the door. Georgie had planned on this and as Dutch's shoulders breached the entrance, Georgie let go of the ropes and watched as the solid wood door came crashing down on Dutch, knocking him unconscious and pinning him face down to the ground. It all happened so quickly that Dutch had no time to even grunt as the door collided with the back of his neck.

Madeline stepped back in shock not quite knowing how to process what had just happened. She looked across at Georgie whose heart was racing, staring at what she had just done. Both their eyes met and neither of them knew what to do next. Out in the cave entrance, Thomas and Dominik were both on edge for different reasons. Thomas thought Georgie was about to try and run out straight into the line of fire and Dominik feared his chances of getting rich were starting to slip away. He pressed the gun firmly on Thomas' temple and snarled 'Don't you move, or I'll shoot your stinking head at point blank range, stay down!'

Thomas stayed motionless staring at the door, praying Georgie knew what she was doing.

Georgie reached down and checked Dutch's pulse, like her father had shown her so many times on him before. To her relief, he was alive. Madeline snapped out of her initial shock and was now back to her poisonous self.

'You stupid little witch! I needed him!' Madeline yelled.

'Well too late Ms Wolf, you're going to need me instead.' Georgie replied coolly, dusting herself off and straightening out her clothes.

'Whatever you're after back there, I'll help you get it. But when we get back out front, make sure French boy out there disposes of the gun over the cliff and you let my dad I walk safely away.' Georgie now held an advantage.

She had presumed there was to be some heavy lifting in the caves and that's why Madeleine had hired someone like Dutch to work for her. Georgie had decided that taking out Madeline's biggest asset would be an advantage for her and her dad's escape. One down she thought, two to go.

Madeline admired Georgie's valour and looking down at Dutch pinned to the floor with blood trickling from his nose she knew Georgie was right. She wasn't going to let things go in Georgie's favour however. Madeline would make good use of her until at the last moment, with Georgie too preoccupied with her father, she'd strike at her with the flick knife she had concealed inside her jacket pocket. But for now, they had a discovery to make and much to Madeline's surprise it would be with a twelve year old girl stood at her side.

'Let's make this quick then Girl. Here, light these, Dutch has a lighter in his hand.' Madeline said.

She threw two handmade torches toward Georgie and they chimed on the ground in front of her. Constructed out of wood, with cloth dipped in kerosene wrapped around one end, Georgie reached down and prised the zippo lighter out of Dutch's grasp. Igniting the Zippo lighter, she lit both torches as they lay on the ground. She slipped the lighter in her trouser pocket and picked up the flaming torches, handing one over to Madeline. The flames were fierce to begin with as the kerosene helped to ignite the cloth, but they soon settled into a comfortable burn and Georgie was amazed at the amount of light they provided in the cave.

'Well I've got you this far, lead the way.' Georgie said.

Madeline didn't hesitate, she turned her back on Georgie and headed straight into the caves with her torch held high lighting the way.

The caves were enormous, far bigger than Georgie had anticipated. They had been walking for nearly five minutes when they came across their first find. Dressed in rags, a fully decomposed skeleton lay abandoned on the cave floor. Madeline paid no attention to it, simply stepping over it as she marched forward.

Georgie had no idea what they would discover in the caves and was starting to think that the door was difficult to open for a reason.

'What are we searching for down here exactly, it looks to me that all we're going to find is death.'

Madeline laughed 'Haven't you figured it out yet you silly girl? Treasure. Pirate treasure! Keep following the mark of Wolfgang on the walls, it's leading us straight to it.' Madeline replied navigating her way through the cave's passageways.

As with outside the door, Klaus' family cross guided the way, painted on the walls. Georgie had an idea that something was hidden there but had almost ruled out the idea of treasure as it seemed too implausible.

'How exactly do you know that; how did you know about this cave it was pretty well hidden?' Georgie quizzed Madeline, much to her annoyance. Madeline stopped and turned to face Georgie holding the torch close to her face.

'I know what's here because it's my birth right Miss Rivers. I discovered a book, a diary of my pirate ancestor Klaus Wolfgang. Who for reasons I won't explain to you, stowed his hoard of treasure in these caves and never returned to retrieve it. Now less of the questions and let's keep moving.'

'But what about that body, what if there's more, doesn't that concern you?'

'He was shipwrecked here over two hundred years ago, I'm guessing some of his men died here from injuries, or I don't know… starvation, forget about it let's keep going!' Madeline had had enough of Georgie's questions and continued to march through the caves.

It wasn't long before they came across more skeletons draped in rags. This time three piled on top of each other as though someone had intentionally stacked them there. Their skeletons had become intertwined with each other as they had decomposed over the years. It was difficult to distinguish where one skeleton began and the next ended. Georgie knew something didn't add up. Madeline's ancestor would have surely buried or disposed of the bodies more sympathetically if these were his crew, his shipmates. She didn't like what they were seeing. She thought back to her favourite movies and stories of Egyptian treasures she'd read about in magazines and books that ended up being tainted or even cursed for the person who discovered them. Whatever they were searching for she didn't like how this adventure was developing. She thought about her father back at the entrance of the cave and tried to think just how she was going to outsmart Madeline and Dominik to get them both out safe and in one piece. Looking at the skeletons piled on top of each other, Georgie didn't want that to be the outcome for her and her father.

As Georgie caught up with Madeline, she was stood at the beginning of a man-made bridge no more than twelve feet long. It was spanning a dark crevice that looked like it fell far into the depths of the Earth. Beyond the bridge, were what looked like four large wooden chests. It was hard for Georgie to see clearly, with the light starting to fade on their torches.

Madeline didn't hesitate and stepped onto the bridge quickly with both feet desperate to reach what lay on the other side. Georgie was too late, she cried out 'No wait!' but as she called, Madeleine's legs broke through the bridge and her body plummeted through the weak wood spraying chunks of wood and splinters as it burst. She reached up with the wooden torch in her hand. It hooked around the supporting ropes as she fell, giving Madeline a temporary handle to stop herself falling further. Frantically clinging on for her life dangling from the bridge, she screamed out. Georgie felt conflicted, all she had to do was push on Madeline's hands and she'd see the last of her. But she couldn't do that, as much of a monster this woman was, Georgie could never let someone die. She gripped onto the post of the bridge and stretched her arm out for Madeline to lift herself up. Georgie's shoulder felt like it was being pulled out of its socket as the woman heaved herself frantically to safety. She knelt on the ground in front of Georgie, clawing her breath back. She was shaken and embarrassed and found it difficult to be seen as weak in front of Georgie.

'This doesn't change anything.' she said, with a diffident tone.

Georgie stood up and pulled Madeline to her feet ignoring her comment. Using her torch to inspect the bridge, Georgie asked Madeline to support her waist as she crouched down and peered underneath. Georgie's initial suspicion had been correct, the beams of wood used for support were tainted, rigged to catch a person out as they had with Madeline.

'It's a booby trap, some of these plinths are hollowed out and thin. It looks like the dark wood beams are the solid ones, they are laid every two. Only step on the dark beams.' Georgie stood back up and looked around the floor of the cave. She found a discarded piece of timber and passed her torch to Madeline.

'Here, hold this I have an idea.'

Madeline watched on as Georgie used the piece of timber to knock on the parts of the bridge she thought were safe. It looked as though she was correct, every piece of wood she could reach sounded solid as the timber knocked hard against it. Madeline couldn't help but be quietly impressed.

'Well done, you make a far more competent explorer than me. It's a good thing I'm already wealthy. Now cross over and check your theory is correct.'

Georgie ignored the back handed compliment and hesitantly reached her foot out over the broken slats to reach the solid wood. She closed her eyes as the wood creaked under her weight, pressing down onto the bridge. Holding onto the ropes either side, Georgie opened her eyes and looked down, relieved she hadn't fallen through. Madeline smiled as she watched on as Georgie made her way across, being careful not to tread on any of the rigged wood. Once Georgie had reached the other side, she turned back the torch to light the way for Madeline.

Madeline crossed with ease and they both focussed the light ahead of them, tucked into a corner of the cave lay four wooden chests that looked like they had been there forever. Madeline waved the torch across them staring at them in awe, her face glowed in the dim fire light and Georgie could see the look of glee oozing from her. The diary was correct, Klaus had abandoned his treasure here all those years ago. Georgie felt uneasy, there was a strange sensation around the chests and the hairs on her arms stood to attention like she was statically charged. It almost felt like there was an electronic hum around them also, but there couldn't have been this deep into a rock cave she thought. Madeline reached out and opened the chests one by one, letting Georgie open the last one closest to her. She noticed it had been damaged by a blade. The chests were half full of doubloons and jewels and in the one closest to Georgie lay an ornate gold box.

'Yes! Finally, I have it all!' Madeline was maniacal as she forced her torch into Georgie's hand and plunged her hands deep into the chests containing the jewels, feeling them in her fingers, playing with them and caressing them while laughing aloud. She reached into her jacket pocket and pulled out a walkie-talkie. Putting the device close to her mouth she pressed the talk button and spoke.

'We have it, I'll be bringing it out in the next ten minutes. You'd better be nearby.'

Georgie was confused by the order, it didn't sound like she was talking to Dominik, she knew he was nearby. Who was she talking to?

A static reply came through the walkie-talkie 'I'll be there.'

'Who is that?!' Georgie demanded.

'Oh, you'll see dear girl, you'll soon see.' Madeline replied, deliriously laughing and staring at the riches in front of her.

From her cargo combat trousers, Madeline pulled out two folded cotton sacks and handed one to Georgie. Madeline started to fill hers with as much as she could carry before instructing Georgie to do the same.

'Grab that gold box and anything else you can fit in too, we'll come back for the rest.'

Not wanting to anger Madeline, Georgie reached down and picked up the heavy golden box and placed it into the sack, then poured ancient gold coins, necklaces, bracelets and jewels on top. Georgie's heart began to race once more, and she started to feel light headed. She had been through a lot and put it down to signs of exhaustion. Madeline had an evil look about her as she watched her fill her bag and Georgie noticed she was staring at her with a crooked smile.

As Madeline and Georgie made their way back through the caves, Georgie noticed her hands beginning to feel sore. In the darkness of the cave it was difficult to see, but she could swear that blisters were starting to form on the backs of her hands. The sack of riches that she had draped over her shoulder felt heavier with every step she took, and she wondered if she'd ever make it out at all.

CHAPTER THIRTEEN
THE CURSED CAVES

Mr Weaver's legs burned as he rode into a pay and display car park close to the beach, he was having difficulty keeping up with Chinook and called him back to his heel as he slowed to a stop. Resting the bike down he could see Chinook was keen to carry on, through the fence and up to the cliff fronts above. Mr Weaver needed a break, riding a bike so fast at his age hadn't done his body any favours and he tried to remember the last time he had ridden a push bike, struggling to remember. As he leaned against the fence trying to ease the aches in his body carefully stretching his legs, Chinook barked excitedly at him, eager to continue and find Elliot. Mr Weaver got the sense they were close by reading Chinook's body language, but he needed a moment to recover from chasing the German Shepherd across the unfamiliar town. The dog had been busy concentrating on his mission up until now, but all of a sudden, he looked more playful and almost happy. Elliot has to be near he thought, his legs would have to rest later. Mr Weaver looked down at Chinook and nodded pushing himself up off the fence to follow.

'Come on then boy.' he said.

High up above on the cliffs, Elliot had been lying in the long grass studying the black 4x4 up ahead for the last ten minutes. He was about to build up the courage to get up close to the Land Rover when he felt the weight of Chinook pressing down on him, nuzzling his nose into the back of his neck and growling in a low rumble.

'What are you doing here boy?!' Elliot was relieved, as confident as he thought he was being, he had felt very alone and frightened when he arrived at the cliff front seeing the black 4x4 ahead of him.

He looked up to see Mr Weaver standing above him in the moonlight. The old man he hardly knew looked like a superhero standing above him.

'How did you find me?' Elliot asked.

Mr Weaver knelt down low next to Elliot as he began to talk softly.

'I used to work with German Shepherds during the war. They were my favourite dog, I loved and lost many of them at the hands of the Waffen-SS. Chinook led me right to you, didn't you boy?' Mr Weaver ruffed up Chinooks fur on his chest and the dog rubbed his body along Mr Weaver's back, he seemed to hold a charm over the dog and they acted like old friends around each other.

Elliot noticed Mr Weaver never touched or patted Chinook's head and thought he'd hopefully get the chance to ask why at some point. But right now, he was more concerned about Georgie.

'Georgie is down there. There's a cave just off the cliff hidden behind a waterfall, it's a bit of a tight walkway but if you hold onto the rope and walk single file it's easy enough to get to.' Elliot said.

'Okay lad. I'm going to need you to stay on guard next to their car with Chinook for me. The police will be on their way soon and I'm going to need you to tell them where to go. As for this cave, can you show me the way?' Elliot nodded and they both set off with Chinook proudly walking in between them. Mr Weaver had no clue as to what he was going to come up against in the cave, but he wasn't going to stand by while Georgie and Thomas were in trouble.

Dominik was growing impatient, he was tired of standing there holding a gun whilst Dutch was injured right in front of him. He had no idea what was happening in the caves. He ordered Thomas to back up towards the wall where Dutch had installed the climbing anchors. He secured Thomas to one of the pitons using the cable tie around his wrists and placed the gun on the ground next to Dutch. He put his head down close to Dutch and could hear that he was still breathing, but he knew the weight of the door pinning him down wouldn't be good for him. Dominik tried to lift the door by hand, but it wouldn't budge, the pressure on his legs made his injured ankle complain and he lacked the strength to get the door to move alone. He looked around the cave, he knew there were crowbars nearby. He spotted one near the equipment they had brought. He grabbed it, jamming it under the door in an attempt to raise it once more. This time it did move a little and Dutch started to groan, encouraging Dominik to keep trying. Behind him Mr Weaver slowly walked through the waterfall getting completely soaked through, the water was freezing but he kept his composure. He saw Thomas tied to the wall and noticed the shock on his face when he realised who was walking towards him, Mr Weaver pressed his index finger on his lips signalling for him to stay quiet. Thomas nodded in approval and his eyes focussed down to the gun on the floor. Mr Weaver understood and could see the Beretta.

As he approached Dominik, the nearest weapon he had to hand was a frying pan sitting on a camping gas stove. He reached for the handle and lifted the pan getting closer to Dominik, Thomas could only stand and watch in silence being shackled to the wall. He was worried for Mr Weaver's safety and really couldn't understand how he was there. Had Georgie got hold of him somehow before they were taken? Mr Weaver got within striking distance to Dominik and raised the frying pan high ready to strike. What Mr Weaver had failed to notice was a fork sitting inside the pan, it fell fast toward the ground. It clanged hard and loud bouncing off the rock surface, the sound reverberating around the cave. Dominik turned quickly to see Mr Weaver ready to attack, without hesitating Dominik lunged for the gun and aimed it straight at Mr Weaver's head firing off a shot. With lightning quick reflexes Mr Weaver dropped the pan in front of his face. The bullet ricocheted off the pan and struck Dominik's plaster cast. The bullet penetrated the cast but stopped just shy of his skin, it was furiously hot, and Dominik could feel it burning his into his flesh underneath. He dropped the gun in pain trying to pull the cast off his leg, screaming in French as he frantically clawed away trying to tear his cast off his leg. Mr Weaver didn't need to think twice he took advantage of Dominik's predicament and brought the frying pan down hard on the top of his head, knocking him unconscious on the floor right next to Dutch.

'That's not the first time I've had to do that.' Mr Weaver said to Thomas with a grin before dropping the pan to the floor. Thomas' heart was in his mouth and he exhaled a huge sigh of relief.

On the opposite side of the door, Madeline and Georgie heard the gunshot. Georgie feeling weaker by the minute dropped the sack of treasure and stumbled toward the rope to lift the door. Using everything she had left, she tried to pull the once easy rope down to open it but fell to the floor exhausted. Crawling closer to the gap to look through, Madeline stood in her way.

'What's the matter Georgie? Feeling a little under the weather?'

Georgie looked up at Madeline who was revelling in Georgie's predicament, she couldn't understand what was happening to her. She was feeling fine, a little battered from the falls she had endured but this, this was different. She felt like she had come down with the worst case of flu she could imagine. Suddenly two crowbars chinked into the ground under the door and Georgie heard two voices that lifted her spirits.

'Georgie! Hang on sweetheart, we're coming to get you!'

Out on the top of the cliff guarding the Land Rover as Mr Weaver had instructed, Elliot was certain he had heard the faint sound of gunshot and was starting to panic. He ran around to the back of the car looking towards the car park hoping to see the flashing blue lights of the police. There was nothing, then as he turned back to keep a watch on the cave he could have sworn he saw a hooded figure drop down over the cliff. He rubbed his eyes and shook his head, he must be seeing things he thought. He ran over to peer down to the walkway but saw nothing. Chinook sniffed at the grass and crouched down ready to protect his owner, Elliot knew he wasn't seeing things. Someone had just snuck past them and was heading towards the cave.

Madeline hid in the shadows as Thomas and Mr Weaver raised the door high enough to allow Thomas to roll through to Georgie. He saw the ropes for the door and pulled them down opening it as wide as it would go. He tied the ropes around the pulley to keep the door open, allowing as much of the spot light in from outside. He dropped to his knees and painfully lifted Georgie up to his chest, he could see she was in a bad way and blisters were covering her hands and neck. As he dragged her out to Mr Weaver and into the light he couldn't understand what was happening to his daughter, she was trying to tell him something. He put his ear close to her mouth.

'Don't touch the treasure, something… not right…' as he turned around to see what Georgie was talking about, he saw Mr Weaver walking towards them clutching a bag.

'No! Drop the bag!' Thomas yelled.

Instantly Mr Weaver let go with gold coins and jewels spilling over the cave floor, a gold box bounced out from the bag landing close to Georgie's feet. It spilled open and a decorative Egyptian amulet in the shape of a bird rolled out onto the floor. Madeline Wolf stepped forward from beyond the cave door laughing quietly, Mr Weaver reached for the gun aiming it at her while stepping in front of Georgie and Thomas for protection.

'Well, well, well, the little explorer figured it all out. That's the cause of your pain right there Georgie Rivers. Stolen from the Pharaohs of Egypt more than three thousand years ago, it's been causing its owners a fair bit of bother since.' Madeline's English was impeccable, but her German accent was thick as she viciously hissed her words at them.

The day's events had started to take its toll on Madeline and she was beginning to become delirious. She was desperate to escape with her riches and be done with all the interruptions of children. As she sauntered out from the door she glanced down at Dutch and Dominik, incapacitated on the floor and spat at them before hissing the word 'Useless'. Dutch had started to become conscious but chose to stay where he was and listen.

Mr Weaver held the gun up pointing it at Madeline, but his arms began to feel heavy and he could feel himself beginning to sweat. Madeline reached down slowly in front of Mr Weaver and lifted up Georgie's sack from the floor. She extended her index finger, pointing to the gold amulet.

'That amulet once belonged to many of the Egyptian Pharaohs, until it was stolen from the Pharaoh Hemeda by the imposter Pharoah Ammon. He had managed to overthrow Hemeda and take his reign for over a year before Hemeda could once again regain his throne, being the rightful heir and ruler of Egypt. Before Ammon was overthrown, he managed to hide a wealth of artefacts from Hemeda which he planned to flee with if he was ever conquered. Unbeknownst to him if the treasures ever left the land of Egypt with someone not of rightful descent, they supposedly would become cursed and bring nothing but misery to its owner.' Madeline sidestepped, inching her way closer to the waterfall.

Thomas looked down at the amulet and then to Georgie suffering in his arms, Mr Weaver began to cough, and Thomas could see he was struggling to stand up. Thomas refused to believe in curses as much as he refused to believe in fairies and ghosts, but the evidence in front of him was staggering. His daughter lay almost lifeless, his friend was starting to show signs of weakness. As he searched his mind for logical answers, he was painfully aware that the only possible explanation was that Madeline was telling the truth.

'For the last five years I studied and investigated what brought my Greatest Grandfather's ship to lay at the bottom of the ocean. It took me that long to decipher what treasure he had stolen from another ship The Good Grief all those years ago. Hours of research, years of speculation, a broken marriage… yet look, it appears I was correct. That amulet is indeed cursed, and it was destined for the two pathetic jokers lying on the ground unconscious next that bloody door! Outsmarted by a little girl and a geriatric. Looks like they got off lightly, if your daughter hadn't got involved Mr Rivers it would be Dutch and Dominik currently suffering the torment of the amulet, while I escaped with the rest of the haul. Pity for Georgie and the old man. I did have a contingency plan if things didn't exactly go my way, but unfortunately for you, it looks like he's a no show.'

Madeline stopped talking and clutched the cotton sacks close to her chest to start to run, she didn't get very far. Dutch had reached across and grabbed her by the ankle, stopping her from leaving.

'I knew you'd double cross us, you're going nowhere! Georgie I'm so sorry please…' as Dutch tried to apologise to Georgie, Madeline smashed her bag of treasure down hard into his face rendering him unconscious once more.

'Pathetic.' she said, as she kicked away his hand from her leg.

She turned and started to make her way to the waterfall, as she got close to her escape a shiny blade penetrated the water. Behind it followed a tall cloaked man whose face was hidden inside a dark hood pushing her back into the cave.

'You, you made it! I thought you had changed your mind? Put that thing down right now, why are you pointing it at me? It's over there, it's all yours!' Madeline was surprised to have a sword pointing directly at her jugular, she was rattled, after a confident speech she now sounded afraid and unsure.

The figure removed his large black hood that fed into a long heavy cloak, it hung down near to the floor and he held out a bronze Khopesh sword that was curved at the front and looked dangerously sharp. He was a rugged Egyptian man with chiselled features, piercing blue eyes and black tattoos of what looked like Egyptian text on both his cheeks. Staring down at Madeline, he signalled for her to move further back into the cave with a movement of his sword. He pressured her back almost all the way back to the door. Georgie was only just able to still process what was happening and her eyes caught the mysterious man's as he approached them.

'You let a child touch the amulet?' he asked, in deep accented voice.

'I didn't ask her to she grabbed it herself!' Madeline was showing signs of vulnerability and her confidence was fading.

The man, still holding the sword at Madeline, knelt down next to Thomas and put his hand on Georgie's hand. Madeline grimaced as she watched on. Georgie tried to speak but the man stopped her.

'My name is Gahiji, do not worry child, you will be okay.'

He stood up and returned his sword into its scabbard while staring at Madeline, she was motionless not knowing what to say or do next. Mr Weaver was struggling with his strength but still managed to keep the pistol pointed at Madeline. Gahiji scooped up the golden box and amulet, ignoring Georgie's attempt at a warning. As soon as the amulet was in his hands the static noise that it seemed to emulate dispersed and a pulse of energy exploded through the cave. The blisters on

Georgie's hands started to heal back to her normal skin, almost immediately she began to feel better. Mr Weaver too noticed his symptoms subside and felt his strength returning. Placing the amulet back into its box and feeding it into a pocket inside his large cloak the man began to speak.

'I am one of the last of The Medjay, the protectors of the Pharaohs. I am reclaiming this amulet in the name of Pharaoh Hemeda and will return it back to where it belongs, with its people in Egypt and I release you of your suffering. I will also take the rest of the artefacts you're holding Ms Wolf, they too belong to the people of Egypt.' Gahiji returned his focus to Madeline, who uncontrollably started shaking her head.

'No, no that wasn't the deal. When I found you all you wanted was the amulet? These are mine, they belong to me! They're my birth right!' As Madeline ran for the waterfall Mr Weaver fired the gun at her, hitting one of the sacks causing jewels to erupt all over the floor of the cave.

Madeline burst through the waterfall clutching onto the remaining sack and Georgie leapt to her feet feeling almost human again.

'We can't let her get away Dad, they killed Simon!' Georgie shouted, Thomas was still trying to process everything that was going on and was struggling with his injuries. Georgie didn't hesitate and ran after Madeline.

'No Georgie, wait!' He called, as he painfully got to his feet and chased after her leaving Mr Weaver with Gahiji.

Elliot heard the gun fire and glanced toward the waterfall, he could see a woman desperately trying to claw her way along the ledge of the cliff face. He knew she was the woman Georgie had described from the petrol station. Almost immediately behind her, Georgie burst through the waterfall and saw Elliot.

'Elliot stop her, don't let her get away!' She shouted.

Elliot knew what to do, with a sharp and quick whistle Chinook was right at his side. As Madeline climbed up to the surface she turned to be greeted by Chinook, staring her in the eyes. Elliot was stood behind and casually said.

'Sic 'em boy.'

Chinook burst into his ferocious performance, leaping up on his hind legs viscously barking in Madeline's face. With his saliva spewing into her eyes, she dropped the sack of jewels behind her losing them over the cliff and cowered back toward the Land Rover, kneeling down protecting her face. Georgie climbed up behind her, satisfied that Elliot had her pinned down.

'I knew you'd be here!' Georgie grabbed Elliot hugging him with all her strength, 'Look it's the police!' Georgie pointed in the direction of the car park as flashing blue lights were visible, producing the reassuring silhouette of the police running towards them.

Thomas and Mr Weaver now appeared behind Georgie, relieved to find her in one piece with Madeline cowering on the floor being held hostage by Chinook.

'Hey, where's Gahiji?' she asked.

'He ran out ahead of us, is he not up here?' Thomas said.

Georgie smiled, whoever Gahiji was he sure was a mystery and she loved that. As the police approached, Georgie filled them in and gave a thorough statement. She explained how she had suspected the three visitors were up to something and that she knew they were guilty of foul play towards her dad's old friend Simon Jenkins. The two men she explained were incapacitated in the hidden cave. Thankfully Mr Weaver had tied them both together to stop them attempting an escape if they came around.

The police confirmed they had found Simon dead in his van, deep at the bottom of Northshore's largest lake after his wife reported him missing. Divers were currently attempting to recover his body. Even though Georgie knew they had done something to Simon the truth was still hard to swallow. The paramedics soon arrived and started to treat Thomas' injuries, as he had started to struggle with his breathing. Georgie knew he would probably spend the night in the hospital, maybe even her too as she had taken quite a beating at the hands of the cave. She stood looking out to the sea with the moonlight shimmering over the waves.

'Sorry Klaus' she thought, 'You lost out again.'

Without warning, Madeline broke free from police custody with only one hand securely locked into her handcuffs. Pushing the arresting officer aside. She tore the flick knife out from her concealed pocket, flicked it open with menace and started to charge at Georgie, screaming at the top of her voice.

'Damn you Georgie Rivers! Damn you to hell!'

There wasn't enough time to react and Elliot was too far away to help, Georgie was stood alone and exposed, Madeline was less than a meter away and about to hit her with all her force. Georgie did the only thing possible and leapt out of the way just as Madeline was about to hit. Madeline swiped the knife at Georgie missing her by inches slicing her shirt. Madeline had gone too fast and couldn't slow herself in time, she plunged off the edge of the cliff screaming all the way to the sea and rocks below. Georgie landed on the cusp of the cliff top clawing onto the grass to stop herself falling over the edge. Elliot ran towards her with his arms outstretched ready to grab onto her, but it was too late. As the grass tore from the ground, Georgie fell backwards over the cliff. She held her breath not knowing what else to do as gravity pulled her body over the edge. With her eyes closed tightly she started to fall, but for only a second. She felt a jolt in her midriff, Gahiji was stood on the ledge gripping onto her climbing harness with one hand and holding onto the cliff with the other. He pulled her up to safety, then quickly covered his head with his hood and crouched down low into the cliff ledge, his dark cloak making him almost invisible to the people above them.

'So that's how he does it.' Georgie said.

Thomas had been through hell and the sight of his daughter safe and sound on the ledge of the cliff face was enough to bring him to tears. Everyone cheered when they found her there safe and as they all pulled her to safety busily commenting on how lucky she was, her secret saviour quietly slipped past them like a ghost. But Georgie knew, Gahiji looked back and gave her a thankful nod before he disappeared into the shadows.

Mr Weaver pulled out Tracey's phone number from his pocket and looked at Elliot.

'We'd better let your mother and Edith know we're all okay. They're probably worried sick' he said.

'We'll help you with that sir, we'll take you and the boy home. Is this your bike lad?' one of the police officers responded.

Elliot was worried he was in trouble and wasn't sure what to say when Mr Weaver quickly interjected.

'Yes, it is. One of those criminals had stolen it from him, can we please load it into one of your vans and safely get it home for him? I believe Elliot left his mum's push bike down by the car park also.' Mr Weaver winked at Elliot and the police officer called over a colleague to help him load the bikes into one of their vans. Georgie and Elliot looked at each other and laughed.

Georgie grabbed hold of Mr Weaver and squeezed him as hard as she could, with tears forming in her eyes.

'Thank You for coming after us, I knew you'd understand what was happening, all I could do was call your number and hoped you heard what was happening. Good old Mickey Mouse!'

Mr Weaver looked down at Georgie and smiled, wiping away her tears with his finger.

'Anytime kiddo, you've started your own adventures now. Just make sure you share them.'

Mr Weaver gave her a kiss on the top of her head and made his way toward the police van. Elliot was left there with Chinook at his side staring at the ground. Georgie could sense something was wrong.

'Are you okay El?' she asked.

Elliot looked out to the ocean, he was trying to find the words but found it hard to get started. Georgie held his hand and smiled, he relaxed.

'I should have come over sooner, I could have helped somehow, called the police sooner, I don't know. But I should have been there, I'm sorry.' he said.

Elliot felt heavy with guilt, he nearly lost his best friend only two days after meeting her and the realisation was proving difficult for him to deal with. Georgie knew straight away how he was feeling and knew he wasn't being rational.

'When my mum was diagnosed with cancer I blamed myself. I don't know why, it was her body, her life. But somehow, I thought I was the cause of it. I blamed myself for all the arguments we had and all the times I had chosen to do something else rather than spend time with her. I made a point of spending every available minute I could with her towards the end, pained with guilt. It only did one thing, nothing. It did absolutely nothing but make me feel lousy. I was there the day she passed away and I remember she looked at me with all the love in the world and I felt it. That's when I realised you can't always be there, you can't always get it right, but if someone loves you that's okay, that never changes. Whether it's your mum, dad, or a friend across the street. It's okay. You weren't to know we were followed home any more than I was to know my mum would get cancer. I'm just sorry you didn't get to see the treasure.'

'Treasure?!' Elliot's eyes lit up and Georgie knew she had lifted some of the weight off his shoulders.

'Loads of it El, in massive treasure chests! Not to mention the cursed amulet that nearly killed me, oh and the booby-trapped bridge. I can't believe you rode the KX down here, I'm well impressed!' she replied.

'What?! Wait a minute, where's the treasure now? How did you get across the bridge?! You were cursed?!'

Georgie chuckled and threw her arm around Elliot's shoulders as they made their way towards the waiting policemen and paramedics, filling him in on all the events he'd missed out on in the cave.

CHAPTER FOURTEEN
NEW BEGINNINGS

Two hundred feet below the cliffs, Madeline dragged her aching body out of the sea and onto the sand of the shore. She had been lucky, as she fell the waves had broken her fall and the current had dragged her out away from the rocks. Her neck was sore, and her sides felt bruised as she coughed out the seawater that remained in her lungs. She was desperate for a drink, the salty seawater had made her dehydrated, but that would have to wait. She rolled onto her back into the sand and looked up to view how far she had fallen. She knew she was lucky to be alive, but she was furious. All her efforts had led to this, to nothing. All her research, all the expense, left empty handed because of a stupid girl. She watched on, shivering wet and cold as the blue lights from the emergency vehicles flickered from the top of the cliff. If she was to survive, she knew she had to move and get out of the country before the police tracked her down. Even though it was Dominik who had killed the landlord, she was still an accomplice. The Land Rover was hired, and no doubt being forensically investigated by the police as she lay there. She knew she couldn't head back to Northshore, it was too risky, the cash she had stashed there would be taken as evidence.

The police would also find the photographs of the caves, the copies of Klaus' journal and her belongings back at the unit. Her fingerprints and even DNA would be recorded and kept on file, she'd have to be more vigilant in the future. She had no doubt that Dominik and Dutch would have no problem embroiling and blaming her for all the events that had led them to being arrested. They'd try and negotiate a deal, a plea bargain, but they were both in a bad way and would require medical attention first. Her passport and clean clothes were waiting for her back at her hotel in the neighbouring village of Sambrook Bay. She was glad she chose to stay out of town and she knew she only had a window of around four hours to escape, back to the safety of Germany. Her mission now was to get to the hotel on foot, without being seen and to head to the airport as quickly as possible.

It was late July; six months had passed since the events at the cave. The weather was warm and clear, and Elliot gazed out across the huge still lake at Brecon Beacons National Park. This was the second time in a year that the school had decided to visit here, and Elliot thought about the last time he was there. He had spent most of the day alone, filling out his questionnaire about the wildlife on a clipboard. He finished the day, quietly skimming stones on the lake before getting harassed and teased by Carl Coombes and Dillon Davies, something he had become very used to. Many things had changed since then, the flowers were in full bloom, the fields were an emerald green and this time he wasn't the only one stood at the bank skimming stones and counting the bounces.

'One... two... three... four.... five-six-seven-eight! Yes! Beat that Cassley!'

Excitedly beating his highest score, Georgie - who was easily and always at least two bounces better than him. Was making this visit on the whole, perfect. They had sat on the bus together sharing Georgie's headphones from her Walkman, listening to the Guns N' Roses album 'Appetite for Destruction'. Elliot hadn't heard of them before and was instantly hooked, he had never heard anything as powerful or exciting and couldn't wait for Georgie to make him his own copy on cassette. Georgie had widened her taste in music ever since leaving Cheltenham, now that she no longer needed to fit in with what society or the other girls in school expected of her. Most of the girls at Northgate were still very much fans of the boy band 'Bros', but that wasn't for Georgie, not any more. After hearing the song 'Paradise City' on the radio one day, she convinced her dad to take her to a record store in Cardiff to buy her the album. She was enjoying being comfortable in her own skin and being allowed to like what she wanted, rather than being influenced by her peers.

Georgie still showed slight signs of the scars to her hands and legs from the events in the cave six months before. At times, she could still feel the burn of the blisters on her skin and occasionally found herself looking down at her hands, expecting to see them once more. The slightest memory of that November night, a smell, an emotion, even just the weather brought back the sensation of pain and the suffering she felt at the hands of Madeline Wolf. But as time went on, the flashbacks were fading and thankfully so were the scars. Elliot threw his last stone of the day, it looked promising and he thought he was onto a winner. But he only managed seven bounces, giving Georgie the status of 'The Ultimate Champion' as she called it, throwing her arms high in the air.

Life at school had improved greatly for Elliot once Georgie had started. News spread fast around Northshore and embarrassingly, Ms James held a special assembly introducing her to the school as a hero of Northgate and a pupil everyone should look to emulate. Elliot found he became Georgie's personal security for a time, having to stop many over eager pupils from bombarding her with questions of how she thwarted gangsters, solved a murder and discovered age old pirate treasure. Georgie wasn't fazed by the attention, she knew it would eventually die down and her story would soon become just that, a story.

Georgie and Elliot had tracked down and met Simon Jenkins' wife Karen and his children. Karen had been so thankful to Georgie for trying to find out what had happened to him and felt some closure knowing that the criminals who had killed him were behind bars. The trial for Dominik and Dutch was scheduled for a few weeks' time and Georgie was a key witness. Thankfully because of her age she would be protected from the media and would remain anonymous to everyone outside the courtroom. She wasn't looking forward to being face to face with the men once again, but she'd have her dad and Mr Weaver by her side, so she knew she'd be okay.

The teacher yelled out for the pupils to return to the bus for the journey home. As they approached the bus Carl Coombes and Dillon Davies were blocking the door. Elliot's heart started to race as he expected the usual trouble. But as they got closer to the entrance of the bus, the boys simply stepped aside paying them no attention. Things really were different for Elliot now and he was starting to enjoy life in Northshore a whole lot more than when he had first moved there. The walk home from school now took considerably longer for him, as he and Georgie would casually chat about their day and plan what activity they wanted to do on the weekend together. Georgie had started to teach Elliot how to climb and toyed with taking him out onto real rock soon, there was no shortage of rock to climb in Northshore. But Elliot had promised Georgie some long overdue motorbike lessons and that was the plan for the coming weekend. He was now confident riding his Kawasaki KX alone and after hearing about the danger his son had faced, his dad had started to play a more active role in his life again. He visited every Sunday to spend time with Elliot and Alice and recently managed to get Elliot's old bike back up and running for Georgie to use with him in the playing fields. One thing Elliot was thankful for after the business at the caves was getting a small part of his dad back. Even if it was just one day a week, he was comfortable in the knowledge that his father did actually care about him and his sister.

As Georgie and Elliot strolled into their estate they were greeted with a familiar picture. Thomas and Tracey casually chatting outside Elliot's house looking very relaxed in each other's company.

'I've always wanted a brother.' Georgie said.

'But I've already got a sister, I don't need another one.' Elliot replied with a grin and they both laughed.

'I still find it hard to believe my mum doesn't remember being in school with your dad, you sure he's not a spy or something?'

'She's two years older than him, he just wasn't on her radar I guess.' Georgie said matter-of-factly and saw Chinook bounding his way towards them barking happily. He'd always rub his body along Elliot first, but swiftly nudged his nose playfully on Georgie's hand encouraging a fuss. Thomas' face would always light up at the sight of his daughter and even more so after witnessing her so close to death in the caves. He'd struggled to let her out of his sight after he was released from the hospital with two broken ribs and a partially collapsed lung. Thankfully his colleagues at his new surgery had rallied around them, helping with transport to and from the hospital. His injuries had delayed him starting at the surgery by a couple of weeks, but he had soon become the town's favourite doctor and he was happy to be back in the swing of things after so long away.

The police had informed Georgie that they never found a body for Madeline Wolf, but they were confident that she had likely washed out to sea. Many forensic experts had deduced that her chances of surviving the fall were very slim. Georgie was more interested in where Gahiji had gone and if he was exactly who he said he was. She couldn't have been more thankful to him, he saved her life twice in one night and she never got the chance to thank him before he disappeared into the night. He said he was returning the treasure back to the people of Egypt and she hoped it would show up in a museum someday, especially the amulet. As dangerous as she knew it was, it really was a beautiful piece of craftsmanship and it deserved to be admired she thought, especially if it had once been the property of the Pharaohs.

'Hey you two!' Tracey shouted.

Thomas raised his arm and welcomed Georgie with a hug.

'So how was the school trip guys? Manage to stay out of trouble?' He asked.

'Yeah it was good, I noticed plenty of crag's for climbing up there dad, we'll have to all go up one weekend. Show Elliot the ropes. No pun intended!' Georgie said enthusiastically laughing. It had been a long time since Georgie felt happy. She ached for her mother constantly but now she felt a shimmer of hope that she could miss her, but still enjoy her own life.

'Sure thing, sounds good. Hey, I reserved a video with Ray earlier in the week and picked it up this morning. How about we bring it over later and have a movie night together?' Thomas said.

'Great what's the film, anything good?' Tracey asked.

'Oh, it's boring really, the kids won't like it... Back to the Future 2 or something...' he winked at Tracey.

Georgie and Elliot jumped for joy, they had both missed it in the cinema and had been desperate to see it. It was agreed, they would all see out the end of the week at Elliot's and Georgie couldn't be happier.

Life in Northshore finally started to settle down into something pretty close to normal as Thomas and Georgie walked over to their house. Thomas squeezed Georgie's shoulders into his side, he was proud of his daughter and how well she was dealing with things. She had put up with a lot of horrific things in the past year, losing her mum, getting kidnapped and coming perilously close to death herself. The last six months had seen them rebuild their lives into a new normal and even though it hadn't gone quite to Thomas' plan, things were looking good for the future.

'Mr and Mrs Weaver are going to pop down tomorrow night, I told them we'd visit them instead, but they insisted. I think they're missing you more than they thought they would.'

'The one thing I miss from back home is having them nearby, it'll be nice to see them. I bet Mr Weaver has told everyone of our little adventure story at the bowls club every week, for the last few months.' Georgie laughed.

'Oh, and probably at the post office, the pharmacy and the coffee shop. He's probably told the milk man too!' Thomas grinned, 'But I wouldn't have it any other way, we owe them a lot.'

As they walked into the house together Georgie glanced at the Mickey Mouse phone and smiled. His nose had been broken off in the struggle. Her dad had managed to super glue it back on, it was a little wonky, but it added to the charm she thought. Georgie threw her school bag under the stairs and kicked off her shoes ready to settle into the weekend. She had been desperate to get home and get into comfier clothes than her school uniform. As she ran upstairs her dad called up to her.

'I forgot to mention you've had a letter delivered today, it's down here on the kitchen table.'

A letter? That's strange she thought, she wasn't expecting anything. Maybe it was something from the courts or the police in relation to the case? Hopefully it wasn't some silly fan mail from a pupil at school again. Although, her dad was pretty good at spotting those and disposing of them. After getting changed back into her usual uniform of jeans and a loose t-shirt, she returned downstairs to check the letter. The envelope was ivory in colour, the paper was thick and felt expensive. Her name was written finely with a fountain pen as Miss G. Rivers, followed by her address in deep blue ink. Looking at the postage stamp it featured the word Deutsch and instantly Georgie knew it wasn't from the UK but Germany. She reluctantly turned the envelope over and slid her finger under the top flap, tearing at the wall of the envelope. Peering inside, it contained a single sheet of ivory paper. Hesitantly she removed the paper and unfolded it, reading the solitary line of handwritten text in the middle of the page.

I know where you live.   MW.

Georgie's heart was racing, her mouth went dry. She screamed for her father and he rushed to her side taking the paper from her hands. He glanced at it before dropping it down on the table. Looking at Georgie trembling, he held her in his arms.

'It's probably a prank sweetheart, a sick joke by a kid in school. I'll call DCI Lewis and get them to take a look. Please don't worry about this, she can't and won't hurt you ever again. I promise.'

He meant every word. Since Georgie's ordeal he'd had an alarm installed at the house and extra security locks fitted to the doors. At home he knew she was safe, but he also knew he couldn't watch her or protect her every move outside of it. Georgie felt sick, she thought she had seen the last of Madeline Wolf when she watched her plummet from the cliff. But she was still alive. She had managed to survive somehow and now Georgie knew what she wanted, revenge.

'I know it's not anyone from school dad, I've never told anyone her name. This would have taken a few days to arrive here, she could already be on her way for all we know.'

Georgie was right, a woman of Madeline's intellect would find some way to gain access back into the UK from Germany. If she was smart enough to escape the last time, then no doubt she'd get back in just as easily. But Georgie was defiant, she sniffed back her tears and straightened herself out standing upright free from her father's embrace and looking him in the eye.

'Let her come dad, we'll be ready for her. I've beat her once before, I'll do it again.'

One hundred and eighty miles away, arriving at Gatwick airport on a direct flight from Salzburg, Austria. A high-class businesswoman watched on patiently as her bodyguard ploughed through the busying people to collect her luggage off the carousel. She removed her sunglasses and produced a counterfeit Austrian passport for the customs officer. He looked at the attractive blonde-haired woman as she smiled at him and quickly compared her to the photograph on the passport. Satisfied with his checks, he stamped the passport saying, 'Enjoy your stay madam' and handed it back. She thanked him and slid it into the front of her handbag as she walked away from the desk. The airport was busy with people leaving and arriving from their holidays and business destinations, but the woman glided through the terminal as though she was the only person there. The last time she visited this country it was for business, but this time she was visiting for pleasure. It had taken her six months to plan her return to the United Kingdom. Trust was something she could buy with the crime syndicates of Berlin and it proved useful when she needed to purchase a new passport and driver's licence. She spared no expense in recruiting the best team money could buy to alter her identity. She had her hair professionally dyed blonde and being a natural redhead, her fair complexion suited it well. A simple change of hair colour and the addition of tinted glasses transformed Madeline Wolf, into Natasha Gruber. With the aid of a dialect coach, she had successfully managed to lose her German accent when needed and replace it with a very convincing south east English accent to help disguise her nationality while she was in England. The passport may have been useful to get her into the country undetected, but she now intended to change her identity once more. Once in England she had arranged for another identity change, with her new documents awaiting her in a safe deposit box.

Her hired driver awaited her arrival outside the airport and the air felt thick with smog. Madeline Wolf had never lost at anything in her life and she was back for revenge. As she stepped into the car the driver received her instructions.

'Head for Cardiff, South Wales. I'm meeting an old friend.' She said.

'As you wish ma'am.' the Essex driver replied. He raised the privacy partition, put the Mercedes into gear and pulled away.

Madeline kicked off her stilettos and sat back to relax, knowing she had a three-hour journey ahead of her. There was only one thing on her mind as she lay there with her eyes closed. How she planned on bringing a painful end to Georgie Rivers.

Printed in Great Britain
by Amazon